CAN'T FIGHT THIS FEELING

LIBBY WATERFORD

ALSO BY LIBBY WATERFORD

Sawyer's Cove: The Reboot

Take Two

Take a Bow

Take it All

Take a Chance

Hot Take in Steamy Shorts: A Kissed by Romance Anthology

Take Another Look in A Kiss at Midnight: A Kissed by Romance Collaboration

Never a Bride

Can't Help Falling in Love

Can't Make You Love Me

Can't Fight This Feeling

Can't Hurry Love

Weston Reunion

Flirting with Her Professor

Her Reunion Fling

Falling for Her Ex

For Truman and Holden

CHAPTER 1

KATE'S INBOX

From: Nicole Winesap <nicole@winesap.design>
To: Rosie Snyder <r_snyder@venturahospital.org>; Kate Treanor
<kate@treanorpod.com>; Lani Kalama <lani@winesap.design>;
Ophelia Winesap o.winesap@clintonelemen.edu

Subject: Three weeks out!!!

Hey you Beautiful Badass Bridesmaids!

Crunch time, ladies. Three weeks until the big day. You should have received communication from René about your final dress fittings. If you haven't, let me know ASAP.

Honestly, almost everything is set, so I just need you to hang in there a little longer. Also, it's not too late if you want to bring a plus-one. Lani? Kate? I can definitely find someone to escort you for the evening if you're into it. No pressure! :-)

Have I told you all lately how much I love you? I couldn't have done this without you. I'm so #blessed to have you in my life <3 <3 <3

Kisses,

Nicole

* * *

KATE

Did you get Queen Nicole's latest decree?

ROSIE

Oh yeah. That reminds me, can you give me a
ride to the dress fitting tomorrow? My car's in
the shop and Gus has to work.

Gus working on the weekend?

My workaholism is rubbing off on him.

Sure. Pick you up at 11. Unless you're worried
about getting whatever weird thing I have. I
don't think I'm contagious, but…

Symptoms?

Super tired, sometimes feeling like I'm going
to throw up, but then not. Dizzy.

Headache?

Sometimes.

Could be stress-related. Are you under more
stress than usual right now?

OK, dumb question. We'll all feel better
after the wedding's over, right?

Only 3 more weeks!

You could always go to your doctor, get a blood test. You're probably due for a physical anyway.

True.

Drink water. Get some sleep and see how you feel tomorrow. 

CHAPTER 2

KATE

I'm on my hands and knees under the desk in Studio C when my wireless earbuds start ringing, startling me into bumping my head on the underside of the desk top.

"Damn."

I rub the sore spot on my head, shuffle backwards on the industrial gray carpeting, then click to accept the call. I answer with a professional, "This is Kate," but barely get it out before a frantic, high-pitched voice pierces my eardrums.

"My wedding is in three weeks! I am freaking out. I need you to talk me down."

Nicole. I wince at both the knot on my skull and the fact that I didn't screen before picking up.

"Nic, I'd love to talk, but I have a recording session this afternoon, and a bunch of deadlines."

"Sorry, sorry. I know you're busy." Nicole's voice lowers in contrition. "But Rosie and O are working, and Lani says I'm not allowed to talk about the wedding at the office anymore, and my mom just makes me more crazy. You're my rock, Kate."

That's me. Move over, Dwayne Johnson, because I'm The Rock. The one with infinite reserves of strength. The person my family and friends turn to when they need a head check. But lately, what used to make me strong seems to be making me brittle. As if I've been slowly splintering ever since Ben died.

I sit back, suddenly both dizzy and exhausted. If I didn't have to produce a podcast in ten minutes, I'd curl up under the desk and take a nap. Which is strange, because the last time I took a nap I was in kindergarten.

I sigh and give myself over to the inevitable. "It's okay. I have a few minutes. Talk fast."

Nicole launches into a ramble about Ricky's godparents and hotel accommodations and a dozen other details I don't need to know about. *She* doesn't need to know about them, but she can't help herself. Micromanaging is one of her defining traits.

She's been like that since we met. Nicole was a blonde, perky freshman living down the hall from me, a redhead with similar tastes in TV and music. We looked like sorority sisters, and together we slayed. Nicole's still as perky as ever, while life has hardened my edges a bit.

I pull myself up off the floor and lock the studio before heading to my office at the end of the hallway. I grab the half-drunk green smoothie off my desk and take a sip. The familiar taste usually centers me, but today my stomach roils. I set the cup down. "Honey, why don't you take a break from wedding stuff and get a massage or something?"

"I suppose I could do that."

"Ricky's godmother's problems are not your problems. She shouldn't even be bothering you with them."

"I just want everything to be perfect." Nicole's voice is small, and I soften. She's a micromanaging Bridezilla, but she's *my* micromanaging Bridezilla.

"You are going to have the most sensational wedding of the decade," I say. Because it's true. She's put so much time and energy into planning and designing her wedding, it's practically taken on a life of its own. It's even being documented for one of the Santa Barbara bridal magazines. "But, sweetie, it's not going to be perfect. Things are going to go wrong. The important thing is that you and Ricky are getting married." I have to take a deep, steadying breath so my voice doesn't crack. "Everyone you love is going to be there. And there's going to be cake. Everything else is just...icing. And not that bullshit fondant. Buttercream."

She laughs and I know I've gotten through to her. "You're right. No one but me cares about most of this stuff. I just...I want it to be *spectacular*."

"There's no way it won't be."

"Thanks, Kate."

"Of course," I say briskly. "Now I have to get back to work."

"You work too much."

"I can't help it if I'm the most in-demand podcast producer in L.A."

"Yeah, you are. You should hire an assistant."

I wrinkle my nose. I've been hearing that for months, but I haven't been able to find the time to think about it, much less do it. "True. Now go book that massage."

"Okay. I'll see you tomorrow."

"Tomorrow? Oh right, the dress fitting."

"Noon. I'll make sure there's lunch. Byeee." She makes a kissing noise over the phone and ends the call.

After that whirlwind, I'm exhausted again. What is the matter with me lately? For a couple of days in May I thought I had a stomach flu, but then I felt better. Now I'm tired all the time. My friend Rosie, fellow bridesmaid and real-life doctor, thinks I should get a physical, but I haven't had time to make an appointment.

Before I can even jot a note to remind myself to call my doctor, Jay, my engineer, pokes his head into my office.

"The lights in Studio B are strobing again. Can you call the landlord?"

I groan internally. "On it." I click through my contacts and text Hakop about the lights.

Maybe I do need an assistant. With the slate of shows I've signed on to produce this year, my fledgling company can afford it, but it's hard to imagine sharing my workload after carving this business out of nothing but my own determination.

Nicole's not the only one who has a tendency to micromanage.

I shake off everything—my fatigue, my nausea, the wedding —so I can do my job. Ignoring how I feel in order to cope in the here and now, that I'm pretty good at. I hustle back down the hall to Studio A, praying that the mics and the lights are both working fine in there.

Jay has already fitted the two hosts of *Brew O'Clock* and their guest with headsets. The guys are bantering, warming up. Each episode they bring in a case of local beer and its brewer and proceed to work their way through the case, starting off by asking questions about the brewmaster's process and veering off on comedic tangents. Everyone gets shitfaced by the end and it's all very entertaining.

"Hi guys." I wave to Kushan and Vern, who wave back. I offer my hand to their guest. "You must be Mike. I'm Kate Treanor."

"Hi, Kate." Mike O'Dowd owns one of East L.A.'s most successful craft breweries. He shakes my hand, his grip strong. His broad shoulders are encased in a tight-fitting T-shirt with his brewery's logo emblazoned on the front. "Nice to finally meet you."

"Likewise. Glad this finally worked out with everyone's schedules."

He smiles at me, brown eyes crinkling. I turn away quickly and lean over the table to verify the mic hookups, even though

I'm positive Jay's got everything set. When I stand up and look back, I'm pretty sure I catch Mike checking me out. Huh.

"I've never done a podcast before. I'm a little nervous," Mike says. "Got any tips?"

"Don't worry, Kate always makes us sound good," Kushan says. "We were clueless before she took pity on us and became our producer. She saved us from ourselves."

I appreciate the praise, but clearly Mike needs more concrete help. "Don't stress. Pretend you're in your tasting room and you're talking to some customers about what they're drinking. It's just a conversation."

"What if I'm boring?"

"That's where these guys come in." I point to the hosts. "Their job is to keep it moving. We'll cut out any dead air in the edit. And don't worry, the alcohol helps."

When all the technical stuff is triple-checked, I give them the green light to begin. Kushan and Vern were inexperienced when they approached me with their idea, but they've gotten really smooth at the whole thing a year into it, and their audience grows every week. You wouldn't think that many people care about the Los Angeles craft beer scene, but *Brew O'Clock* gets hundreds of thousands of downloads per episode, and since the subject matter is ready-made for advertising, it's my most profitable podcast by far.

The two-hour taping drags on, even though Mike is, of course, not boring at all. In fact, he's witty and personable and passionate about his product, and I can tell this is going to turn out to be a great episode. Unfortunately for me, the smell of the IPA they're drinking is turning my stomach. I usually don't mind nursing a cold one while we tape, but today the idea of alcohol is even less appetizing than my green smoothie. I'm relieved when we wrap and Jay gives me the all-clear sign.

"So, we're going to grab some dinner," Mike says, gesturing at Vern and Kushan, while I'm packing up. "You free to join us?"

I look at him for a second without answering, then find my voice. "I can't. Yeah. Sorry. But thanks."

"Okay," he says easily. "Maybe some other time."

"Maybe."

And then they're gone and Jay's doing his thing. I retreat to my office. I have to finish packaging and uploading two shows by midnight, though if I focus it shouldn't take me nearly that long. My stomach grumbles uncomfortably. I open the mini fridge and grimace at the options. Sparkling water or the rest of the smoothie. I pick up the cup half-filled with spinach-green liquid and sigh. Smoothies aren't food. You can't sink your teeth in and chew. But when Ben's monthly subscription box had arrived a week after his funeral, I didn't have the heart to cancel it. I've been choking down this goop ever since.

I get the first file ready and hit the upload button when my phone chimes. I have the sense to screen this time—but it's just a text.

LANI

What did you say to Nicole? She actually left
the shop early and went offline.

> I told her to stop worrying about every little
> detail and get a massage.

And she listened to you? I wish I had that
superpower.

> She listens to you.

Only about work stuff. Anyway, thanks. She
needed that and I'm enjoying the peace and
quiet.

> You still at work?

Leaving soon. You?

> Same.

Hey, so I think I got asked out tonight.

Tell me everything.

Just a guest on Brew O'Clock. He asked if I
wanted to get dinner after the taping. Like a
group thing, but also not, you know?

Sure. Hot?

I guess? I mean, yes. I don't think I'm
interested.

Clearly not, or you'd be out with hot beer guy
and not texting with me from work on a Friday
night.

But it was weird, I sort of thought about being
interested. Which is new for me.

Well, you know what I say—go for it. Just
don't forget the pact.

I would never forget the Never a Bride pact.

Good, because we're the only 2 single ladies
left and I don't want to be the last woman
standing.

Don't worry. Dinner is a long way from 'til
death.

I look at the last word on my screen. Three years ago, I
wouldn't have qualified to be a Never a Bride(smaid), because I
was about to get married. Then Ben had to go and get himself
hit by a car biking home from work and I essentially became a
widow before I got to say "I do."

Ever since, I've worn figurative widow's weeds. I haven't
even wanted to meet anyone new. My fellow bridesmaids and I
started our tongue-in-cheek Never a Bride "club" as a way to

link arms against the force of Nicole's matchmaking machinations.

Okay, so the name was my idea. I was scared that all that wedding hoopla would send me back into the darkest days right after Ben died, when I had to simultaneously make funeral arrangements and cancel wedding plans. The Never a Bride club was a way for me to stay strong, to pretend it didn't get to me, to keep being the rock that Nicole and everyone else needs me to be.

Tonight was the first time I've wanted to take a guy up on the offer of a sort-of date in a very, very long time. It's not like I haven't felt the itch. I even scratched it—once, and a touch recklessly, not that long ago—and ever since, it's been harder and harder to know what I want. Is it good to want to go out to dinner with a cute guy? Does that mean I'm ready? Intellectually I know I have to try it to find out. But I'm scared.

It's been three years—both forever and not nearly long enough. I don't know if I'll ever be ready. But I know that if Ben could see me, running from a simple dinner, running from life, he'd be disappointed in me.

I don't know how to be ready. But I have to believe that I will be, someday.

Just not today.

CHAPTER 3

KATE

Saturday I have to drag myself out of bed, even though I went to sleep earlier than usual. I plop a green tea bag into my favorite travel mug and skip breakfast. Nicole always goes overboard with food, so I figure I can make it up at lunch. There's not much traffic so I pull into a parking spot on Rosie's quiet residential street in Ventura almost an hour ahead of schedule.

I could text and warn her, but I have to pee like crazy, so instead I knock loudly on the door of Rosie's new house. The house itself isn't new—it's an attractive postwar wood frame on a corner lot. She and Gus bought it jointly. They've only been together since the fall, but when his lease was up they decided to pool their resources and buy something big enough for Gus to have a garden and a greenhouse in the back. Even though they haven't mentioned babies or weddings, they did get a house with plenty of space in case they end up with a small roommate one of these days.

Gus answers the door wearing pajama bottoms and nothing else, leaving his impressive chest tattoo on full display. I think, not for the first time, that Rosie lucked out getting a guy as fine as he is kind. "Hey, Kate, come on in."

"Hey, Gus. How's tricks? Actually, hold that thought—can I use your bathroom?"

He points me in the direction of their guest bath. "I'll let Rosie know you're here."

Business complete, I follow the voices through their sunny living room to the back of the house, where the kitchen opens up onto a patio absolutely covered in potted plants of every size and seemingly every possible shade of green.

Rosie sits at a wooden patio table, pointing at something on her phone. Gus leans over her shoulder, smiling at her softly instead of whatever's on the screen. He's got it bad. I shove down the brief flare of jealousy and pull up my own chair.

"Hey, girl." Rosie looks as sleep-disheveled as Gus, in yoga pants and a loose breast cancer awareness 5K shirt. I briefly wonder if by being early I interrupted sexy times.

Ugh, no need to go there, though of course I'm happy for Rosie. It's wonderful to see her relaxed and content. As long as I've known her—almost fifteen years now—she's always been Type A to a T, focused on her dream of being a doctor, always letting her social life sink to the bottom of the priority list. Since she met Gus, things have been different. She seems happy, which makes me happy.

"Coffee?" Gus asks.

"No, thanks." I can't help making a face at the thought. Coffee's another thing I haven't been drinking lately. The smell is too overpowering.

"I'm going to get dressed," Gus says, dropping a kiss on top of Rosie's head. She waves him away, her cheeks pinking up at the display of affection. God, they're disgustingly cute. They're everything I used to have. Everything the Never a Brides are supposed to disdain.

"Sorry I'm early," I say, to get my mind off this depressing train of thought. "I couldn't eat this morning, so I just got in the car."

"You couldn't eat? How else are you feeling?" Rosie asks, her focus shifting smoothly to me. She's a great doctor because she makes people feel heard, makes them feel taken care of. The relief of being around her is enough to make me a little teary. I'm not against crying, but only when I have a good reason.

"I don't feel great, but it's nothing major. My appetite has been off. I slept ten hours last night. Ten!"

"Well, you don't look sick." She looks me in the eye, asks me to open my throat and shines her phone's flashlight back there. "I could take your temperature, but I don't think you have a fever. I wonder..." Her mouth does a funny little twisting thing, as if she wants to smile, but doesn't know if she should.

"What?"

"Sweetie, when was your last period?"

I freeze as the implication of the question hits me like a punch to the solar plexus. Why hadn't I thought of it before? "Oh no."

"Kate?" Rosie looks concerned at whatever expression has broken out on my face. Something between horror and confusion, I expect.

"How could this not occur to me?" Seriously, I'd considered mono, flu, allergies, even psychosomatic illness. I had not considered *pregnant*.

"When—"

"Bachelorette party," I croak. It's hard to breathe. My chest tightens with the familiar beginnings of a panic attack. I haven't had one in maybe a year, but my body sure as hell remembers what it feels like to be so overwhelmed it starts shutting down.

"Honey, breathe." I hear Rosie's voice from far away. She's by my side, rubbing circles on my back, pushing my head down between my knees. "Breathe. It's okay." She keeps talking, murmuring in my ear about how she's there and she's not going anywhere, and I focus on her voice, soft, gentle, patient.

Fuck me. I'm pregnant.

I suck in a ragged breath—the first full one I've gotten in what feels like an hour, but I know it's only been a minute or two. Slowly, I raise my head, and my breathing slows. My heart still feels like it's going a mile a minute.

"Better?" Rosie's calm, but her forehead creases with worry.

"The night we went dancing. I went home with a guy."

"That was what, six, no, seven weeks ago? You haven't had a period since then?"

I think hard. I'm usually regular, but I guess I haven't been paying attention. "No. Should I take a pregnancy test?"

"You should definitely take a test, but my official doctorly opinion is you're pregnant, Kate." She says the words softly, as if she's not sure how I'm going to react to the news. Fair, since I just wigged out on her.

"Wow." My head swirls with a jumble of emotions. I latch onto the first one I can. "I'm actually relieved. I thought I had developed some obscure fatigue syndrome that no one would believe I had."

"Once you're out of the first trimester, your symptoms—the fatigue, nausea, headaches—will likely go away. But you're definitely going to want to schedule an appointment as soon as possible with your OB."

"Right. Okay." My OB is a middle-aged Scandinavian woman who's been my doctor since I was old enough to start going to the gynecologist. She's also my mother's doctor.

Oh God. My mother.

"Rosie. How am I going to—" I look at her helplessly. There are so very many ways I could end that sentence.

"Whatever you want, you'll figure out how to do it. Okay? I'll help you."

"I know you will." I look down at my hands. The backs are as Irish-pale as the rest of me, the palms red from where I've been rubbing them on my thighs. My fingers are bare. I took my engagement ring off a couple of years ago when the diamond seemed to be mocking me every time it winked in the light.

I always wanted a family, to be a mom. But this wasn't how I ever imagined it happening. After Ben was gone, I tried not to think about the fact that having kids was no longer an option.

I've known I'm pregnant for about ten minutes, but that's about as long as I've loved the tiny, surprising life inside me. Ten minutes into having my world shaken up in the most petrifying, wonderful way possible. It doesn't matter that I don't have a ring on my finger. The baby won't care.

"I'll call my doctor, but can I take a pregnancy test anyway? Like, right now?" I need to know for sure that I'm not going crazy in a new, innovative way by somehow making all of this up.

"Okay. Do you want to go to the hospital with me? I can give you a test there."

I loathe hospitals. "No, one of those pee ones is fine. Right? They work?"

"They're very accurate," Rosie confirms. "But I don't have any. Want me to go buy one?"

"Um." I don't want to be left alone with my thoughts. "Could Gus get it maybe?"

"Sure, if it's okay to tell him."

I'm under no illusion that any of this isn't going to be making the rounds among the Never a Brides and their significant others by day's end anyway. "Yeah. It's okay."

She nods. A mischievous smile crosses her face. She yells, "Gus!"

He pokes his head out of the patio door after a moment's delay. "What's up, hermosa?"

"Can you go to the drug store and get a pack of pregnancy tests?"

His mouth drops open and Rosie cackles. "For Kate!"

His mouth closes and he sags against the door. "Oh, Jesus. Don't do me like that."

"Sorry, I couldn't resist!"

Even I let out a small laugh. "Sorry, Gus."

"For real, you need…" He looks from Rosie to me and grins when I nod. "Sure. Give me ten minutes."

He disappears and Rosie's still laughing.

"Wow, you are cold, Rosie Snyder. I didn't know you had it in you."

"I know. We've talked about kids—very hypothetically—but we're not ready. Still, I just couldn't pass up that opportunity."

"Fair."

We sit for a while, the sound of birds and cars on the street outside filling the silence.

"How are you feeling right now?" she asks eventually.

"Besides being shell-shocked? I feel like an idiot for not even thinking that I could be pregnant."

"And aside from your ego being bruised, how do you feel?"

I say the first word that pops into my head. "Happy."

Her face, which had been studiously devoid of emotion, relaxes into a smile. "Yeah?"

"Happy. Scared. Overwhelmed, yes. But I'm—I don't need that stupid test to know it—I'm going to have a baby."

"Oh, Kate." Her eyes are full of tears, but I know they're joyful ones.

"I've imposed on you enough for one day—with the free doctor advice and scaring the shit out of your boyfriend and everything—but I have another huge ask."

"What is it?" She looks so elated for me she'd say yes to anything.

"This dress fitting today—I'm going to have to tell Nicole I need my dress adjusted. I could barely button my jeans this morning."

Rosie's eyes grow wide as it sinks in how big of a deal this is going to be. "Oh, I don't know."

"Please. You said you'd help me."

"Yeah, I meant medically or emotionally. Not telling Nicole you aren't going to fit into your dress. I don't have a death wish!"

"Come on, please?" I use my rusty acting skills to make my blue eyes big and round and pleading. I blink, doe-eyed. She sighs, and I know I've won.

"Fine. But you're going to tell her *why* you need your dress refitted, right? She's going to know something is up."

"If I tell her, won't it take away from the wedding specialness?"

Rosie bites her lip, thinking. "I think she'd be more hurt if you kept it from her."

I sigh. "You're probably right. Fuck. I'm going to have to tell her sometime. At least maybe she'll be so excited about the fact that I'm pregnant she'll overlook the dress-fitting part?"

Rosie laughs. "Yeah, that might work." She grabs my hand, squeezes. "You're going to have a baby! I can't believe it!"

"Me either," I say. Only, in a surreal way, I can.

"You might not want to talk about this right now, but the guy—you're going to tell him, right?"

Oh yeah. The guy. The blurry image of messy black hair and dark eyes swims through my head.

"Of course. I need to tell him."

There's just one problem. I sort of don't know who he is.

Nicole Tiffany Winesap and Richard James Kendell, along with their parents, invite you to celebrate their union in matrimony

Saturday, June 20
Five O'Clock in the Evening
Rancho del Sol
Santa Barbara, California
Reception to Follow
Formal Dress

CHAPTER 4

OLIVER

Three weeks later

A river of brake lights greets me as the 101 winnows down from three lanes to two just past Ventura. I stab the call button on my steering wheel in frustration. A single ringtone echoes in the cabin of my Mercedes and then Nat picks up.

"What?"

"I know I'm not supposed to call you on your day off, but remind me why I'm going to this wedding again?" It's been a long week and I still have a million things to do in the office. "There's a ton of traffic. I think I'm going to be late."

Even though riding a motorcycle in my suit would have been impractical, if I was on my bike I could have dodged in and out of traffic. Instead, I'm slogging it out with everyone else trying to escape Los Angeles for the weekend.

"It's a fantastic networking opportunity." Nat's voice comes through loud and clear over the car's speakers. So does her exasperation. "Ricky Kendell is your main investor and not only can't you afford to alienate him, he has an extensive local network. If you want Mercy SB to open big, you need to make sure the locals are lining up to get in, not just the tourists."

"Ricky's a good guy, but I feel gauche going to his wedding when I've never even met his fiancée."

"Nicole Winesap, owner of buzzy studio and retail store Winesap Design. Old-money Santa Barbara family. Graduate of UCLA and Parsons."

"Are you reading her Wikipedia page?"

"I do my research."

I know she does. That's why we're on the cusp of opening the third outpost of Mercy in as many years. When I first got the idea for an upscale gastropub that would exclusively feature local produce, meat, and beverages, Nat's the one who got me interviews with investors, who put together profit and loss sheets, who made me look good when I brought my proposals to the breweries that I ended up making exclusive deals with. Together, we've achieved the rarest of endeavors—owning and operating profitable restaurants.

Sometimes I wonder why she needs me in this partnership. "Eye candy," she's laughingly told me before, more than once. She's not wrong. My face and name have always been my ticket to success. Sometimes I wonder if I hadn't been born Oliver Mercier, son of Aziza Amine, one-time supermodel, and Gerald Mercier, New York City wine distributor extraordinaire, what could I have accomplished on my own? More? Less?

I sigh. There's no reason to be ashamed of my high-achieving family, but I lost my sense of entitlement so long ago they've always been more of a burden than a benefit.

"I should have brought you with me," I say, unwilling to let go of my grumpy mood. I used to view socializing as a perk of my job, but lately it's been a chore.

"I've been your wedding date before and I have better things to do than be ignored all night while you flirt with lonely bridesmaids."

I wince, even though she can't see me. "Sorry about that. But bridesmaids—there's an idea." It's been a couple of months since I've hooked up with anyone, and I cheer at the prospect of mixing business and pleasure.

"Have your fun, but please do not do anything to fuck up this deal." It's like we share a brain and she knows the shortest path to killing my vibe.

"How could I? The paperwork's been signed for months."

"Yeah, but if you accidentally sleep with Ricky's favorite cousin and then never call her again, who knows what revenge he could enact?"

"You know what I love about you, Nat? You always expect the worst of me."

"Then prove me wrong. Be good. Network. And get back to the office in one piece on Monday. We have a shit-ton of work to do before the opening."

"I know, I know. I'll be good." Good's a relative term, after all.

I end the call and finally, *finally*, get off the freeway and into the line of shiny cars streaming into Rancho del Sol, an old California ranchero-turned-event-venue with a grand lawn, mission-style buildings, and spectacular views of the sun setting over the Pacific Ocean.

After handing the Mercedes off to the valets, I'm greeted by a teenager in a suit that looks like it cost more than my own Armani. He offers me a program. My jaw drops as I flip it over. Two-sided. Jesus. Maybe I should have timed my arrival for the reception and used the weekend traffic as an excuse.

A solemn usher, also nattily dressed, shows me to the groom's side, which is filled to the brim with guests who look like an advertisement for a Santa Barbara retirement community—monied older men accompanied by either women who've gone gracefully gray or their blonder second wives. There are more people here than a royal wedding. I find a single seat on the far side and sneak a peek at my email, feeling mildly guilty when the man sitting next to me shoots me a dirty look. I stash my phone, notice that Ricky, the only person I know in this circus, has taken his place at the front of the grand hall, four groomsmen in bespoke suits lined up like soldiers behind him.

The music changes from generic classical to something familiar, though it takes a minute for my ear to place the song—a string quartet version of Beyoncé's "Crazy in Love." Nice choice. I rise and turn with the rest of the guests. We watch as two toddlers bobble down the aisle spreading handfuls of flower petals with pudgy, adorable hands.

As the first bridesmaid struts down the aisle I feel as if I've been teleported to Fashion Week. She's stunning in an intimidating way—iron-flat black hair, ramrod straight posture, flawless tan skin. She rocks her dress—it has fancy cutouts and lacy patches and it's nothing like any bridesmaid dress I've ever seen, down to the color, which is bright orange. No, wait, it's California poppy orange, the exact shade of the state flower that's the focal point of the extravagant bouquet in her hands.

The second bridesmaid, a brunette with an old-fashioned wave set in her long hair to match the old-fashioned mermaid cut of her dress, follows behind. Her lips are painted fire-engine red like a 1940s starlet, and I catch her winking at a Latino guy with a fade sitting toward the front on the bride's side.

The next one down the runway—I mean, aisle—is a tall, statuesque redhead. I'm distracted by the cut of her dress, which is the same color as the others, but much shorter; the wedding crowd has been treated to a mile of milky legs.

I heartily approve of Ricky's soon-to-be-wife's taste in women—bridesmaids, that is—not to mention fashion. I take mental notes to share with my fashionista mother the next time we talk.

Something about the redhead makes me want to take a closer look, but she's already at the end of the aisle and the final bridesmaid is floating down. Her poppy orange gown is a puffy cloud that matches the cloud of blonde hair on top of her head. Her round cheeks are rosy pink and she looks painfully happy —her gaze fixed on the man standing next to Ricky at the front of the room. He's a little taller and a little younger than Ricky and he's beaming back at her just as hard. I mentally cross her and the '40s starlet off the list of hook-up possibilities. Clearly, they're taken. Going after Ricky's best man's girl would be a serious breach of etiquette, even for me.

Nat's voice in my head telling me not to fuck up nearly distracts me from watching the bride. A gasp goes up in the crowd when she takes her place at the head of the aisle, holding a handsome middle-aged man's arm. Her dress is white, but it's not just bridal white. It's blinding, sun-on-snow white, and it drips off her in a million different soft petals. The effect could have made her look like a molting swan, but she doesn't. Instead, she resembles a princess of some forest world, radiant and ethereal, like the first white flowers of spring poking through the diamond-hard crust of late winter snow.

After the fashion show of bridesmaids, Nicole takes her rightful place at the center of the proceedings. Ricky can't seem to stop looking at his bride like she single-handedly cured world hunger and invented 5G. The officiant, a middle-aged woman in a silver tunic, gets the ball rolling and after that I mostly tune out the words. Instead, my attention returns to the redheaded bridesmaid.

She's a contradiction, slim but curvy, firm but soft. Her legs-for-days disappear intriguingly under the tulle skirt of her dress. It reminds me of a ballet costume, though her body is no whip-thin dancer's. Her hair is swept up in a bun, completing the haute-couture-ballet-dancer look, and her eyes, probably blue based on the rest of her coloring, are fixed on the ceremony in front of her.

Then something extraordinary happens. Someone in the proceedings says something to make the room erupt into laughter. I'm too busy watching her to get the joke, but when the redhead's mouth splits into a smile, her white, even teeth on display, her lips stretched out of their serious pout and into something natural and free, it hits me.

I know her.

I slept with her.

And my reaction to seeing her again already has my blood heating. I try to tell myself it's because she snuck out of my bed before I woke up and I'd been inordinately disappointed not to get a third — or was it a fourth? — round in before our time together came to an end and I'm still annoyed about it. But I'd be lying. My breath quickens and my face feels hot because I want her again and tonight's the ideal opportunity for a second chance.

I glance at the program and my memory is jogged further. Most of the names mean nothing to me but the moment I spot Kate Treanor I know that's her. Her name was Kate. Her name *is* Kate. I grin. This wedding is suddenly less of a chore and more of a gift. And I can't wait to unwrap my orange silk-wrapped bridesmaid.

CHAPTER 5

KATE

The ceremony, despite being the nominal reason we're all here, goes by quickly. Nicole's militarily precise preparation pays off because suddenly the vows have been exchanged, rings placed on fingers, and Ricky's planting a surprisingly passionate kiss on Nicole's meticulously painted lips. He comes away with a red-smeared grin, and my chest surges with affection for the man who has stood by Nicole for a decade and still wanted to make her his wife.

They're both smiling like crazy and wiping away tears as they head back down the aisle. I wait, remembering my instructions, until it's my turn to be collected by Groomsman Number Three and escorted back up the aisle.

I'm relieved the most intense part of the event is over. The reception we're about to enjoy will have its share of important moments, from the toasts to the cutting of the cake, but that's not on me. Nicole's got it worked out like clockwork and she wants us, the bridesmaids who helped her every step of the way, to actually enjoy the party.

Which I plan to do the second I can get out of these fucking stilettos. I avoid high heels as a matter of course, since they make me even more giraffe-like, but Nicole insisted I wear them at least for the ceremony. I stashed a pair of ballet flats that I think look even cuter with the ballet-inspired design of my dress in the venue's coatroom.

"You okay?" Rosie asks as I peel away from the group. She's been doing this hovering thing ever since we found out about the baby. My mind still trips over the word, even though I've been living in this new reality for three entire weeks, and I have the ultrasound of a black and white speckled bean on my phone to prove it.

"Fine. Going to change my shoes."

"Want me to come with?"

"I think I can manage." I try to keep my tone even and not yell at her that of course I can get some stupid shoes all by myself. I'm pregnant, not incompetent. But I hold my temper since Rosie has her own reasons for wanting to make sure I'm comfortable and healthy, given the way she lost her mom in a pregnancy-related tragedy. I give her as reassuring a smile as I can and hurry away.

I need a minute to myself, anyway. Before the ceremony we took about a million photos and my face is sore from smiling. Now Nicole and Ricky are off for their turn in front of the camera and this entire months-long ordeal is blessedly almost over.

I find the coatroom and sink down on a brocade chair, letting out a lusty sigh as the weight shifts off my feet. My spine gratefully relaxes for the first time in hours. Maybe days.

My repose lasts for about thirty seconds before the door opens and a man pokes his head inside. My posture goes rigid as I'm suddenly aware that I'm very alone while the rest of the massive group is headed outside to the lawn tents for round one of the evening's festivities—supper and dancing.

The man makes eye contact with me, a small smile twitching on his generous mouth. I feel my brows draw together as I try to place him. He's aristocratically handsome, with a glossy, neatly trimmed beard, his longish black hair swept back stylishly from his face. Where do I know him from? Was he a guest on one of my shows?

"Hey, you," the man says. "I thought I saw you come in here."

It's his voice, deep and melodious, that makes everything click into place. "Oh, shit."

His smile falters at that. "Kate?"

"It's you."

His smile slides back into place. "C'est moi," he says with a flawless French accent. He cringes a little immediately after, to his credit.

I try to laugh but the sound that comes out is more of an unhinged squawk. After weeks of wondering exactly how I was going to track down the guy whose name I only vaguely remember as starting with a vowel and whose address I only have because it finally occurred to me to check my car service app history, here he is, standing in front of me. The way he's looking at me, it's clear he's got hopes that maybe our one-night stand deserves an encore.

Not only am I not looking for a repeat, I have to break the news that our previous encounter has resulted in some permanent consequences. Well, permanent for me. Time will tell how permanent they are for him.

I really need to stop thinking of him as Him.

"And who are you, exactly?"

"Oliver Mercier."

Oliver. Ha. I knew it started with a vowel.

He comes fully into the room and offers me a hand to shake. I take it, his hand large and warm. I suppress the urge to giggle manically again. I've stepped into some twisted fairy tale where my somewhat shaggy one-night stand is in reality a coiffed, courtly gentleman with superb manners and mobile sperm.

I'm seriously going crazy.

I manage to get out my name. "Kate Treanor."

"Short for Katherine?"

"Just Kate," I say firmly.

"Okay, just Kate. This is fate. You have to give me another chance to make you breakfast tomorrow, since you snuck out after I specifically remember you agreeing to stay for chocolate chip pancakes." He's teasing, but there's an honest thread of regret in his words.

"Sorry about—that night was just—" I stop, unsure how to explain the entire clusterfuck in a pithy sentence or two.

He raises his eyebrows. "Spectacular? Earth-shattering? The best night of your life?"

I'm pretty sure he's joking, but just my luck to hook up with an egomaniac with a dimple.

"Not like me," I finish. One-night stands are something other girls do, ones with less baggage and more guts. Girls like Lani can take home a different guy every Saturday night and make it look good. Even before Ben died, spontaneity wasn't really in my vocabulary.

"Oh. And what is like you?" His voice drops to an intimate caress and I narrow my eyes. I remember that tone. That tone got me to throw away three years of celibacy for one completely ill-conceived night of sex.

So to speak.

"Listen, Oliver, I don't know what you think is going to happen here, and I'm not really sure how we ended up here in the first place—"

"I told you: fate," he interjects, smiling at my answering scowl. Dimple alert. *Focus, Kate.*

"—but I'm glad we ran into each other because there's something I need to tell you."

"Okay." His smile dims somewhat. I probably sound like a lunatic. And then I realize I'm about to sound like even more of one when he hears what I have to say. My courage wilts as suddenly as my bridesmaid's bouquet has and I find myself groping for a way out. Lying is definitely the best option.

"I'm—um. I'm late. For pictures. So maybe you could give me your number."

"I'll give you my number if you promise me a dance later."

Dancing is how I got into this mess in the first place.

His eyes twinkle and this smooth, urbane guy is not the guy I remember from bachelorette night—yes, I was drunk, but I remember him as being different. Earthier. Rougher. Stubble and wild hair and plain T-shirt with sweat stains. Even his apartment was college-guy-level messy and cluttered. But if this is the same person, I have to admit the polished version is damn good at flirting.

"Fine." I fish my phone out of my bag and he recites his number as I punch it in, carefully adding his name to the entry. "Mercier." I try to replicate the richness of his pronunciation and fail miserably. "M-e-r-c-i-e-r?" I ask.

"Exactly right."

"I have to go." I take my phone and brush past him out the door, feeling his gaze on me all the way.

"See you later, Kate."

I hum noncommittally and flee. It's not until I reach the lawn that I realize I forgot to change my shoes. Dammit.

CHAPTER 6
OLIVER

I stare after Kate feeling mildly perplexed. What a weird girl. Sure, we didn't actually *talk* much that night, but she hadn't struck me as crazy. Maybe my crazy meter needs an adjustment. Still, even if she's a bit odd, she's still as alluring as she was when I first spotted her in the nightclub all those weeks ago.

I'd taken a few days off work to go camping with my friend J.T. and I came back early, having slept poorly on our trip. Too much fresh air. Too little cell service. I needed a distraction—noise and people and maybe some vodka.

I dumped my stuff at J.T.'s, grabbed a quick shower, and went to a club I'd been to once before. The music was blaring, it was dark and crowded, and by my second vodka tonic I was feeling mellow. All I wanted to do was dance and get out of my own head.

The moment I spotted her, dancing by herself, eyes closed, totally tuned into the music, I couldn't stop my eyes from tracking back to her. I've always been an appreciator of beauty. My mom was one of the first supermodels and is still active in Manhattan's fashion scene. She always had breathtakingly beautiful friends who'd coo over me; by the time I was in high school, I craved the attention. My parents did the best they could, but they were both constantly on the move, their jobs taking them to Europe or out for lavish, hours-long dinners when they were in the city. When they invited my brother and me to tag along, it was to make sure we were learning about the business that they expected us to join.

So much for that.

I like gorgeous women. Sue me. And Kate was the most gorgeous girl in the club, with her fiery red hair, pale skin, and curves that made my hands ache for wanting to touch. I watched her turn away every man that approached her with a toss of her head. She looked like a queen with all the power of one.

Instantly, I wanted to be the one she deigned to dance with. I wanted to be the one she wanted.

She sent another one away, and she happened to look at me. She caught me looking at her. I let her catch me looking. I smiled. I waited. And eventually, she danced in my direction. They always do. I didn't move. I held my ground. And she didn't say anything, but she nestled herself, her back, against my front, and we fit together as sweetly as I somehow knew we would.

Eventually her friends—they must've been the bridesmaids from this exact wedding—were dragging her away to a different club. I didn't know what to do, which isn't like me. I always know what to do. I only knew I didn't want our night to be over.

"You coming?" she asked over her shoulder, with a voice that could only be described as sultry.

I couldn't nod fast enough. As I followed her girl party to the club on the next block, it occurred to me that though I had thought I'd been the one fishing, she'd hooked me so hard I was tripping over myself to get to the next club. It had lamer music and weaker drinks, but I was grateful to be there, if it meant she'd turn those glowing blue eyes on me and let me wrap my hands around her killer hips.

And now it turns out she hadn't even remembered my name.

Life's funny sometimes.

But a second glass of the exquisite sparkling wine from an obscure small-batch California winery—Papa and Maman would approve of the unconventional choice—soothes whatever blow my ego's suffered by Kate's cool response to our reunion.

The band's playing quick-tempo jazz. When I get Kate on the dance floor later I hope we can catch something slow. I've been up to my ears in work, and I feel the itch to get my hands on a beautiful woman. So Kate's a little odd—the exchange in the coatroom hadn't gone exactly like I'd planned—but it's not forever. Just tonight. And tonight I have a hotel room at the Biltmore instead of squatting at J.T.'s, so we could potentially spend the entire night tangled up in each other. I'd have to peel that bridesmaid dress off her, of course, see what no doubt complicated undergarments she's wearing—

"Oliver, hey!" Ricky's ever-cheerful voice wakes me out of my fantasy as he claps me on the shoulder.

"Hey! Congrats, man."

"Thanks!" He's smiling so hard his face must hurt from happiness. I can't quite imagine being that thrilled to hitch my wagon to one woman for the rest of my life, but it suits Ricky.

"Great party," I add, because we seem to be running out of things to say already. We've only met to talk business, never just to hang out.

"That's all Nicole," he says proudly, and again, I wonder what it would be like to be that much in love. "I want you to meet her. Babe, come meet someone." He pulls Nicole away from her conversation with an older couple, whom she waves to enthusiastically as they drift away.

"Nicole, this is Oliver Mercier. I'm working with him on his new restaurant. Oliver, this is my wife." He emphasizes the last two words like they're precious.

She smiles at Ricky when he says it, her face fond, and I feel like I'm witnessing something sacred that I haven't quite earned. She tilts her head up at me and the moment's over. "Oliver, thank you so much for coming."

"It's an honor."

Her wide eyes sharpen on me. "Have we met before?"

"I don't think so," I answer honestly.

"Maybe I've seen you at your restaurant. Ricky took me to Mercy for our anniversary last year and we had a fantastic time. The caramelized Brussels sprouts! I died!" Her effusiveness is charming, and I'm always ready to receive compliments.

"That's great to hear, thanks. I love anything caramelized."

"Me, too. Have you ever tried caramelized turnips? They are mind-meltingly good."

"Turnips? I'll mention it to the chef. We're trying to stay ahead of the cauliflower trend. Turnips could be next."

"I'd be all for it—cauliflower is so played out."

I laugh at her authoritative tone. She's not wrong. "Totally."

"Well, I hope you enjoy the dinner we have planned for tonight."

"I'm sure it will be memorable."

"Are you here solo, Oliver?" Nicole asks, though I'm positive she knows the guest list by heart and is therefore aware I didn't bring a date.

"All by my lonesome," I say with a wink. Flirting with pretty married ladies is a default mode that I should probably turn off when I'm working with their husbands, but Ricky's talking to another guest and isn't paying attention.

She laughs, seemingly delighted, and pulls me by the arm. "Then I need to introduce you to a few people."

I scan the crowd, looking for a redhead in a tiny dress, but Nicole brings me to a cluster of twentysomethings, none of whom are bridesmaids, and introduces me around. I remind myself that this is my entire purpose for being here and concentrate on the introductions. One's a local florist with an orchid in her hair. Another is a local photographer, off-duty tonight, who I already follow on Instagram. Then there's River, standing out in a bow tie and Buddy Holly glasses, who owns a bar called Denim in the Funk Zone two blocks from Mercy SB. We hit it off immediately, and I do what I do best, winning people over, selling them on my vision, making River glad I'm coming to the neighborhood instead of feeling threatened by Mercy's upscale price point.

By the time we're all instructed to find our assigned tables for dinner, River and I have exchanged contact info and discussed doing a late-summer cross-promotional event. I've tentatively booked the photographer to cover the opening. She says she'll talk it up with her followers beforehand, and I feel like even if I don't make any more connections tonight, Nat will be pleased with my progress.

"How do you know the happy couple?" I ask River as we walk to the board to locate our seating assignments.

"I went to high school with Nicole, when she was Nikki and I was Rachel," they say as we scan the board looking for our names. I point out River's first, a little disappointed to see we're at different tables. "When she and Ricky moved back to Santa Barbara a few years ago, they came into the bar and we started getting reacquainted. Nicole's surprising, you know? In high school I always thought she was such a preppy princess, but now I get that was just a box other people put her in. She's still a princess, but she's also crazy-talented. Have you been to her shop?"

"Not yet." It'll have to wait until after the opening, but I'm looking forward to checking it out.

"It's like fifty dollars for a pillow, but the pillow is so beautiful you're all 'take my money.'"

"A glowing review if I ever heard one."

River smiles. "And Ricky's a nice guy, too, even if he's a square."

I laugh. Square is exactly the word to describe Ricky.

"They're so...happy." I try not to sound baffled, but the longer I spend in this world, the more this true-love thing strikes me as a one-in-a-million rarity. Sure, my parents and my brother are apparently happily married, but I've never met anyone I would even remotely consider tying myself to. I'm thirty-five. Maybe it's not going to happen for me.

River smiles at my tone as if they get it. "Yeah, Nicole and Ricky are the real deal. A lot of weddings in this town are just to show off your status, but with them, it's like they know how lucky they are and want to celebrate it."

"With hundreds of their closest friends," I add dryly.

"Fair. But I think it's more about not leaving anybody out. Nicole is very big on inclusion."

"That's cool." Suddenly I feel very much like the privileged jerk I am most of the time. Mercy's about a certain type of experience—memorable food, phenomenal drinks, impeccable service—but I never thought about who it left out of that experience. People like Nicole and Ricky can afford it without a second thought. But what about the college kids who drink at River's bar or the locals who probably hate the influx of tourists that come to the Funk Zone for a good time?

"You look hungry," River says, snapping me out of my thoughts.

"Oh, yeah. Just thinking. Guess we better sit."

River nods. "See you around, Oliver."

I find my seat without any trouble just as the first course is being served. Predictably, Nicole has done a fantastic job of mixing up the crowd, so there are some Winesap cousins from

San Francisco on my left and some Kendell cousins on my right. One of the Kendell cousins is young, cute, and female— in other words, my type. I flirt out of habit but find my gaze slipping more often over my shoulder to the central table where the bridesmaids and groomsmen hold their place of honor.

Kate hasn't looked my way once, but I still feel like there's an invisible string between us, getting tighter as the night wears on. If we don't get some slack on that string, something's going to snap.

CHAPTER 7

KATE

As soon as we sit down for dinner I wiggle off my heels, push them out of sight under the table, and sigh audibly. Barefoot feels a thousand times better.

"I thought you changed your shoes an hour ago," Rosie says as she glances at my swollen feet.

I grimace. Why can't my friends ever let anything go? Like, ever? "I got sidetracked."

Luckily she's distracted by the arrival of the salad course, which she eats while moaning in ecstasy. Gus, sitting on her other side, watches Rosie with undisguised hunger.

I avert my eyes from the whole spectacle, looking down at my plate. I barely taste the delicate greens and rainbow beets. Nicole has refined and revised tonight's menu into something that could be served at a state dinner, but my appetite is still wonky due to the human being growing inside me. My unsettled stomach might also have to do with the father of this eventual person sitting twenty feet away, blithely eating beets.

I have to tell him.

I chickened out before, and I cannot do it again. Even if telling him is a disaster, I'll still feel better once it's all out in the open, once I know what I can expect from him. If I pull myself together, I'm sure I can persuade him that I've got everything under control and he won't feel any guilt in gracefully bowing out.

I glance over at the bride and groom. Nicole's glowing so hard I'm surprised *she's* not pregnant, but her sparkling aura is the result of pulling off the wedding of her dreams. She gets to go home with her husband at the end of the night, and every night after.

My heart lurches with something like envy. I once wanted what she has. I'd been promised it. And it was taken away from me, hard and fast.

My vision goes unfocused as my salad is whisked away by a server and replaced with the main course.

Hold it together, Kate.

I've held it together for months, ever since Nicole sat me down and said Ricky had finally proposed and she wanted me to be a bridesmaid. She'd spoken gently, as if she wasn't sure how I'd react. How could I do anything but smile and hug her and tell her of course I'd be her bridesmaid? How could I punish her for something that wasn't her fault by saying no?

When I told her I was pregnant, barely an hour after the test Gus bought for me confirmed our deductions, Nicole was eerily calm about the whole thing. Maybe giving her something to focus on besides the wedding did her a favor.

We were huddled awkwardly in the waiting room of the high-end seamstress who was adjusting our custom-made dresses. The three Never-a-Brides and Nicole stared at me with what I think they thought were neutral gazes, but what felt like laser beams of intense curiosity. "I want this baby. I want to be a mom," I said. They were so happy. They were less happy when I told them I had no way to contact the guy.

"We'll figure it out," Rosie had said in her reassuring doctor's voice, and I did my best to believe her.

I could tell them right now: He's fallen back into my life,

tonight of all nights. But I don't know how. I don't know how to do any of this, and I'm scared that if I ask for help, it proves that I'm not strong enough to do this on my own. I have to be prepared to do this on my own. All of it.

I only have to keep it together for another few hours, and then I can go to Nicole's, where I'm staying for the weekend to recover from the wedding while they jet away on their Parisian honeymoon. I can't wait to scrub off my makeup and wash my hair and slip into jammies and sleep. Maybe I'll accidentally sleep for seven months and not have to deal with...well, anything.

"Are you finished, miss?"

I look up into the inquiring face of a server, then back down at my plate. I struggle to remember eating a single bite.

"Give her a few minutes," Rosie says.

I glance over my shoulder. He's still there. Oliver. The name sounds strange in my head. I'd been wracking my brains to recall his name and I'd half-convinced myself it was Owen. I'm stalling. I should just get it over with.

"Kate, are you okay?" Rosie asks.

"I'm fine!" I snap. Her head jerks back and I instantly feel terrible. "I'm fine," I say again, more softly. "Thanks."

I get up, not bothering with the dreaded heels. Most of the guests are still finishing dinner, but a few have already migrated to the dance floor. The toasts will start soon, but this can't wait. I march barefoot over cool grass to Oliver's table and wait for him to look up. When he sees me, his smile is abrupt and genuine. It also makes his dimple show, despite the layer of close-cut whiskers on his cheeks.

I put my hand on my belly to steady my nerves, then drop it when I realize it looks like I'm cradling my womb. Ugh. Womb? What is wrong with me? I take a stab at normalcy. "Ready for that dance?"

He lays his napkin smoothly on the table as he rises. "Absolutely."

His hand finds the small of my back and I allow him to leave it there as we make our way to the dance floor. The touch both grounds and electrifies me with its novelty. That's something no one tells you when your fiancé dies: After a while you're desperate just to touch someone, to be touched. Oliver's touch is firm but not pushy.

When we reach the dance floor, the band's playing Dave Brubeck. The tempo is kind of awkward, but we manage to find a rhythm, his hands on my waist, mine around his shoulders. I've taken dance classes all my life, but I haven't met a lot of men who know how to dance properly the way my grandfather's generation did.

But Oliver holds me confidently in his arms—he actually does know how to dance. When he discovers that I do, too, we change positions, our arms sliding into a waltz pose easily. The band, perhaps in response, segues from Brubeck to something that's truly waltz time, and Oliver effortlessly leads me around the dance floor.

We don't talk, mostly because if I open my mouth I'm afraid of what I'm going to blurt out, but it's still nice to just spin around the floor. It's been a while since I danced with a partner like this. The night we met doesn't count. We danced together, but not like this. That was club dancing—dancing as foreplay. That was wanting to feel something pure and uncomplicated. That was the slide of my soft body against his bigger, harder one. It was the scent of sweat, the tang of tequila on my tongue.

When I decided to dance with him that night I wasn't thinking, for once in my life. I saw him and was drawn to him with a primal instinct. And when he touched me I liked what I felt. That hadn't happened to me in so long, I wasn't strong enough to cut myself off.

The longer we danced, the hotter and sweatier we got, the

more I wanted to lick his neck and see if he tasted as salty as the rim of my margarita.

I glance at Oliver's neck. He's not sweaty tonight. He's crisp in a suit that's clearly designer, and I'm having trouble reconciling the two versions of him.

I miss a step when I consider tasting his neck again, sweat or no sweat. He just holds me tighter.

"I got you," he says softly.

This needs to stop. So I do. Right in the middle of the dance floor, I stop cold.

"Oliver, wait. I've got to talk to you."

CHAPTER 8

I grab Oliver's hand and we head for the pool area. The tiled patio is empty. I find a bench tucked in a dark corner and sit him down.

"Okay." I open my mouth, but nothing comes out. I try again. "Remember that night? A couple of months ago?"

His smile can only be described as wicked. "Mostly."

"It was Nicole's bachelorette party and I'd been drinking. Obviously."

"I remember that part."

I pace a little, the Mexican tile smooth beneath my feet. I haven't been this nervous since I auditioned for the Scorsese movie I didn't get. As my nerve weakens, my brain comes up with avoidance tactics. "What are you doing at this wedding, anyway? How do you know Nicole?"

"I don't. Ricky has invested in the restaurant I'm opening next month. He invited me."

"Oh." That makes sense. Ricky's got fingers in a lot of different pies.

"How do you know them?" he asks, as if I'm the interloper here.

"I went to college with Nicole."

"UCLA or Parsons?"

"What? How do you even—"

"Sorry, I'm not a stalker. Just well-informed."

"UCLA."

"Theater major?"

"How did you know?"

"You're gorgeous. I figure you're an actress. Model, maybe?"

I wrinkle my nose at the presumption that my career choices would hinge on my looks. His guess is extra annoying because it's partly true. But Oliver probably meant it as a compliment, so I try to stay neutral. "I did act for a few years," I say finally. "I don't anymore."

"And what do you do now?" He doesn't seem perturbed by the fact that I'm not really an actress, or maybe he assumes I didn't cut it and had to find work elsewhere. Why do I care so much what he thinks, anyway?

"I'm a podcast producer," I say, aware we've gotten really off track now, but I'm not sure how to get back. Instead I sit down on the bench, leaving a few feet between us. Might as well settle in for the long haul. "What do you do?"

"I'm a restaurant owner."

I consider that. I always thought restaurants were hopeless money pits, a place where people dumped cash they wanted laundered for the mob or something. I give him the benefit of the doubt on his being a criminal and narrow my eyes at him. "Family money?" It's my second-best guess.

He straightens his shoulders at that and his cheeks color a little. Shit. I didn't mean to offend him, but it seems my hypothesis hit too close to home. "Sorry, I didn't mean—"

"It's okay. I raised the money for Mercy on my own. Well, with Nat."

"Who's Nat?"

"My right hand. The brains behind my restaurants." The affection in his voice is evident.

"Is he here?"

"She. And no."

Oh fuck. He's in love with his business associate. Of course he is. "And you and she, you're a couple?" I would never have had the temerity to ask this under other circumstances but given that what I'm about to tell him is going to affect him and his relationships, too, I better find out all I can.

He surprises me by bursting out laughing. "Me and Nat? No. I'm definitely not her type."

"Really?" The man in front of me seems like he'd make most girls' lists, between his melting chocolate eyes, full lips, that stupid dimple, and the way he wears the hell out of his expensive suit. I'm sitting here in envy of his silky thick eyebrows, for fuck's sake.

His smile turns into more of a leer as if he can read my thoughts. "She's a breast woman," he says. "I'm more into asses."

"Charming."

Nat may be gay, but that doesn't mean Oliver's not dating someone else. "So you don't have a...significant other?" Far be it from me to assume he's only into women. My assumption success rate has been low so far.

He chuckles. "Would I be here with you if I did?"

"I don't know. I don't know you at all. You could be married with three kids."

"I'm not married. No kids. I don't have a girlfriend. I'm generally too busy to maintain relationships."

The light dawns. "I get it. You're a player."

"That's what you got from 'too busy?'" He looks offended again, though less than he did at the family money comment.

"Pretty much."

"Well..." He shrugs. "Let's just say I date a lot."

"'I'm not a player, I just crush a lot?'"

He laughs. "Sure. Me and Big Pun."

I fight a smile. "Whatever."

"What about you? Boyfriend?"

"God, no." I stick my tongue out in distaste.

He raises the aforementioned perfect eyebrows. "And you're giving me a hard time about being a player?"

I close my eyes and take a deep, centering breath. Five counts in, hold for five, five counts out, just like my therapist taught me. When I open my eyes again, Oliver's looking at me strangely. "What?"

"If you're single, it must be by choice. You are lovely, Kate."

My heart stutters curiously at his words. He's right and wrong at the same time. I've been single for years by choice. But if I had any say in my own life, I'd be with Ben right now. We'd have been married for over two years already. Maybe I'd be pregnant with *his* baby. It feels like I haven't really chosen anything in a long time. I've only been reacting in an effort to survive.

I sigh. None of this is really Oliver's fault, despite the whole it-was-his-sperm thing. As I recall, I was so swept up in the shocking feelings of being touched after so long I hadn't been super persnickety about things like birth control—which I haven't been on since before Ben died and we figured out my cycle well enough to do without.

"Thank you," I say quietly, because there had been a compliment in there somewhere, and despite how unglued I am at the moment, I have manners.

So does Oliver, when he's not being flirtily suggestive. "I'm sorry, I keep interrupting you. You said you wanted to talk to me about something?"

"Right." This is it.

He waits.

I stand up. He looks up at me, face open, expectant.

I sit down. "Okay. Here's the thing."

"Yes."

"The thing is."

"Yes."

"I'm pregnant."

"Oh." He doesn't look remotely shocked enough at those words, apparently thinking this is some superfluous piece of data, like that I went to UCLA.

"I'm not a player. In fact, I haven't slept with anyone in an extremely long time. Well, until a couple of months ago. There hasn't been anyone else."

Oliver's face is comically blank.

"Just you," I prod, hoping he'll finally react.

"Oh," he says again. "So you're saying—"

"I'm pregnant, and you're the father." Maybe I should have led with that.

He smiles, as if I've made a joke, then frowns when he realizes it's not a very funny one. Then he gapes at me for a while. Ha, I've finally cracked his veneer of sophistication, and all it took was an unplanned pregnancy.

"You're sure? I mean, not that I don't believe you." He looks vaguely sick.

I try not to be insulted and put myself in his shoes. Some girl he barely knows springs a baby on him at a wedding they just happened to both attend. Yeah, I could easily be crazy and making it all up.

"Rosie was there, when I took the first pregnancy test. She's a doctor. I thought I had mono or something. Turns out it was just a baby!" I might sound slightly hysterical from the way he's looking at me. "But I guess you'll have to take my word for it that you're the only person it could be, until we get a test done."

"A test. Right. Good idea."

"Or not." Maybe I shouldn't have brought that up. I don't necessarily want him to get attached.

"No, yeah." He looks around, wild-eyed. "You know, when

you lured me to this remote location, I was kind of hoping it was to fool around."

"Yeah." I grimace. "Sorry."

"No, I'm an idiot. I'm just processing. Are you okay? I mean, how do you feel? When my sister-in-law was pregnant, she was sick as a dog the whole time."

I'm surprised he'd even ask. "I'm okay. The nausea and stuff, it wasn't terrible, and now I'm starting the second trimester, so I've been feeling better every day."

"The second trimester? And you only get three?" His voice is strained.

I laugh, because yeah, this is already going by super fast. "Yeah, you only get three. The doctor said the due date is January 2nd."

"So you, you want...this?"

He's being vague but I know what he means. He doesn't just mean the baby—that's only the beginning.

"Yes," I say softly. "Obviously, it was unexpected. But I do. I'm actually happy about it."

"Really?" He sounds curious rather than disbelieving.

It's on the tip of my tongue to explain about Ben, and how I've been so alone, and how this is a chance for me to have a part of that life after all, but the music's stopped and Nicole's father's voice is coming over the sound system. "Shit, the toasts. I have to get back."

I push off the bench, then glance at Oliver, still sitting and looking a bit forlorn. "I know this is a lot. But we can make it easy. Ricky knows a million lawyers. I can have someone draw up something simple."

He frowns. "What do you mean?"

"I'm not going to ask you for anything—child support or help. I'm good to do this on my own. You don't have to worry. But we should probably make it official. Paperwork or a contract or something."

His frown deepens, and I can feel the dinner I didn't eat backing up on me.

"Sorry, you're telling me that I'm going to be a dad, but you want me to sign a contract cutting me out of the kid's life?"

"No! Not exactly. I just—I didn't want you to feel any pressure. I can handle this."

"Maybe let me think about it for five minutes before I waive my parental rights?"

His tone is mild but I still feel shitty. I figured that with his man-about-town demeanor and his admitted playboy tendencies he'd be relieved if I gave him an out. But I don't really know him at all. And now I've just opened myself up to sharing the most important thing in my life with a stranger about whom I know nothing except he waltzes decently and maybe launders money for the mob. Probably not. Still.

"Right. Sorry. I'm, I'm rushing things." I blink back the tears pricking my eyes. I'll never convince him I can do this on my own if I break down in tears over any little thing.

"It's okay." He lets out a gusty sigh. "Shit. It is a lot. You're right. But let's take it one step at a time."

Nicole's dad's voice echoes over the sound system as his speech drones on. I look over to the main tent.

"You need to go?" Oliver offers me a little smile. "Go on. I'll catch up."

I hesitate. We have a lot left to talk about, but obviously we're not going to solve anything tonight. I've got his number, and now I know Ricky can give me more contact information if he tries to ghost me. Or maybe that would be the best thing.

I nod and whisper, "Sorry, Oliver." And I run back to the lights of the reception.

CHAPTER 9

OLIVER

This wedding has gone from being an obligation, to an unexpected opportunity, to...I don't even know how to describe it, but it feels like a bomb has gone off in my brain and I can't chase down a single thought before a new one pops up to distract me.

Kate is pregnant. With my baby. That's probably not very PC, to think of it as *my* baby. I mean, obviously it's hers, too. Ours. But there's got to be something programmed into us that as soon as there's a little being with our DNA out there, we'd do anything to protect it, and its mother.

But the emotion coursing through my body right now goes beyond mere protectiveness. I have a fierce need to stake a claim. Show the world that she's, that *they're* mine. This caveman side of me has me completely unsettled. It's so unlike me to want to stake a claim to anyone.

It's also damned inconvenient, since Kate strikes me as the sort of woman who won't respond well to anything that gives off even a whiff of caveman. I might have thought she was a bit zany or off-kilter before, but now I know she was just trying to cope with this situation. She seems reasonably together, all things considered. She was clear enough about wanting the baby. There's going to be a little human in shockingly few months that I'll have a massive responsibility to.

Because no matter how ardently Kate proclaims she can do this on her own, I have no intention of bowing out.

I cringe when I think about how I didn't waste a breath before trying to pick her up again. And then basically bragged about being a player. God, I'm such an idiot. No wonder she jumped to the conclusion that I wouldn't want to have anything to do with a kid.

Still, she's in an awful hurry to get me out of the picture. What's that about? She could've just not told me at all and I would never have known. But she's got backbone, and guts, to tell me in no uncertain terms that she can do this solo.

I have the overwhelming urge to talk to my father. It's late on the East Coast, but Saturday night he's usually out late, schmoozing and socializing. Wining and dining is literally his business.

My phone suddenly feels like a rock weighing down my jacket pocket. I fumble it out, trying to remember the last time I called my father. On his birthday? A few stilted words, me doing my duty, wishing he didn't sound so stiff and formal on the other end of the phone. Wishing he would say *When are you coming for a visit* or *I miss you* or even just *I love you*. I know he does—that's why he took it so hard when I left. But it's one thing to know it and another to hear it.

I tap the screen before I can change my mind. If he doesn't pick up, fine. I'll deal. I've been dealing for ten years.

It rings. Twice. Three times. Then my father's familiar French-accented rumble comes on the line. His voice makes me think of the lavender soap my grandmother sent by the crate, cakes of which sat perfuming every bathroom of our Upper East Side apartment throughout my childhood.

"Olivier?" My parents are the only ones who call me by my real name. The rest of the world, even my brother Marc, calls me Oliver. I decided around third grade that Olivier was too different and I would only answer to Oliver.

My chest clenches at the way he says it, surprised, as if he hasn't said my name in a very long time. Maybe he hasn't. Maybe it's like I'm dead. Maybe he and Maman never talk about me, even though things are easier with her. She and I talk almost every week. She even gives me advice on the business every once in a while. Last year she came to L.A. and we had dinner. She met Nat, made not-so-subtle comments about my perpetual single status, showed me a million pictures of Marc and Ella's twins, even though I'd already seen most of them.

It's different with Papa.

"Bonsoir Papa. Oui, c'est moi." I start the conversation in French, but I'm rusty and switch into English almost immediately. "Hope it's not too late."

"Something wrong?"

"Does something have to be wrong?" I say, stubbornly not wanting to admit that yes, something is very wrong. My life is about to take a left turn and I'm rather stunningly underprepared for it.

He chuckles at my knee-jerk reaction and I smile despite myself. I suppose I'm not the only thirty-five-year-old who slips back into acting like a teenager around his father. But as I get older, the pattern gets old, too.

"I got some unexpected news and I wanted to ask you—" What? Is he going to tell me the right thing to do? I already know what that is. If I have a child, then I have to be a father to them, even if it's inconvenient. Even if it terrifies me. Kate might think I'm a player, but I don't play when it comes to family.

"You know what, never mind." I vaguely register the toasts going on over the sound system, droning voices occasionally punctuated by laughter. I don't know any of these people, so my guilt at skipping out is short-lived. And these are extenuating circumstances. Finding out I'm going to be a dad doesn't happen at every wedding of a business acquaintance, after all. "Just wanted to say hi, I guess."

"Is something going on with the new restaurant?" Papa sounds concerned. "Investor problems? You're getting close to the opening."

"No, nothing like that. Wait, how do you know about—"

"I have my sources."

Of course, Maman and Marc. Just because Papa and I don't talk doesn't mean we don't care about each other. Suddenly, our tired arguments seem so insignificant.

We're too alike, that's always been our problem. The older I get, the more I understand what that really means—as much as I've been hurting and missing him, he's been hurting and missing me just as much. Probably more.

"Merde, Papa. I've been an idiot. I'm sorry."

He clears his throat delicately. "Are you all right? If it's not the restaurant, are you—are you sick?" He sounds distressed, and I feel bad for making him worry.

"No. I'm fine. It's—" I'm not sure how to explain. It seems premature to tell him he's going to be made a grandfather again. "There's this girl."

"Ah." His voice betrays relief, understanding, and amusement in one eloquent syllable. "La femme. What's she like?"

I'm about to tell him that I barely know her but stop. "She's smart. Tough. Gorgeous."

"So what's the problem?"

"I need to assure her that I'm not a shallow, self-centered playboy. Tall order, huh?" I try to make it a joke, but it's too close to how much my reputation as a dilettante who never sticks with anything still shadows me. I'll never get Kate to give me a proper chance at being a father to our child if she sees me as an inconvenient detail, one that can be swept to the side with the scribble of a signature.

"Olivier, you say shallow and self-centered, but what you have is passion. Your passion is why your restaurants have been successful. You've persuaded people to invest money in your vision, and it's paid off. As for being a playboy, well, Mercier men are all playboys until we meet the right woman."

I can't help but smile at that. I have no idea if Kate is the right woman for me, but I know our lives are intertwined from here on out. She wants this baby, and so do I.

"Through your passion you can convince anyone of anything."

That's usually how I operate. But this is delicate. Kate's not a truculent food vendor or overzealous health inspector. She's a woman with whom I have a very short history, but with whom I want to have a long future. And I have next to no experience keeping a woman around long term, at least one I've slept with. Not that my attraction to Kate is even relevant. She didn't say she wanted to date me or anything.

I scrub my hand over my face. Fuck. There's so much to figure out. But Papa's right— when I truly care about something, I always find a way. I push myself to my feet and square my shoulders.

"Thanks, Papa."

"Of course, son. I'm glad you called."

Now it's my turn to clear my throat awkwardly. "I'm glad you picked up."

"Bien sûr."

"Okay. Bonne nuit." I hang up quickly, the medley of emotions in my chest making me a little unsteady. Things may be changing, but this doesn't have to be the end of my life. In fact, I have a feeling that having Kate in my life is going to take it to a whole other level. Now I just have to convince her of that fact.

I run my hands over my hair, straighten my tie. I desperately want to detour to the bar for a whiskey, neat and strong. But I'm not beginning this campaign with alcohol on my breath. I'm doing this right, or I'm not doing it at all.

I head toward the party. I have a woman to win over.

CHAPTER 10

KATE

"...That's why I'm so overjoyed to be standing here with all of you today to wish Ricky and Nicole a very happy life together, indeed. Cheers to Ricky and Nicole!"

There's much clinking of glasses and "Cheers" and applause as Ricky's cousin and best man Jamie finishes up his speech. Three toasts in and I'm desperately wishing for a glass of champagne to dull the boredom. Not that I'm against all the well-wishing, but there are several more variations on this theme to come, and I don't know how much more I can take.

It rankles slightly that I can't drink. But I'm careful to keep my glass surreptitiously filled with sparkling water in case anyone's antennae are aroused by my lack of alcohol intake. I don't want anyone outside of my tiny circle to know about the baby yet. This is Nicole's night, and I seriously don't want anything to steal her spotlight.

I could have waited to tell Oliver, but seeing him again, it felt like the universe telling me to get it over with before he disappeared again. And it turns out he's doing business with Ricky. Small freaking world.

He took it well. No drama. Not yet, anyway. The thin sliver

of my soul that's not calcified with grief thinks that despite his player tendencies and his shameless flirting and his too-perfect hair, Oliver will end up by being okay with this, maybe even make it easier.

But the hardened lump in the center of my chest that remembers all too well burying the ashes of my twenty-seven-year-old fiancé under the oak tree in his childhood backyard screams there's no way this is going to work out. Either Oliver will be smothering or entirely absent, and I won't get to choose. Again.

God, this night is endless. I clap politely when everyone else does. One more speech, and then cake, if I recall the agenda correctly.

The cake is something to look forward to, anyway. Nicole chose a four-tiered confection with buttercream frosting and a cascade of tiny crystalized flowers adding a ribbon of color. Her taste in wedding cake is as flawless as her taste in everything else. Somehow she makes the traditional feel fresh, combining the comfort of the familiar with amped-up flavor. As much of a pain as Nicole has been over these last months, I do adore her.

Still, I can't lie and say these months of wedding planning haven't been a strain. Every decision took me back to three years ago and my own wedding. Ours was set to be much more modest than this one, of course, because we were younger and poorer, but also because wildflowers and potluck suited us. Ben was a practical dreamer—he was going to make a difference, starting with not owning a car and ending with solving climate change.

When he died, I felt dead, too, if death is nothingness. I was numb. Too numb to feel anything. Not cold. Not grief. Not loss. All of that came later. It still comes, sometimes.

I shake myself out of my reverie. *I got through it.* I got through it, and I'm still here. I'm here and Nicole's here and

Rosie's here and Lani and Ophelia and Jamie, all of the friends I've made through this endless wedding wackiness. I set my hand over my middle and imagine the gentle swell, even though I know to the average eye there's not much to see.

I'm here and I'm not alone.

Rosie catches my eye and smiles. "Okay?" she mouths.

I nod. I'm the rock, remember? The strong one. The one who always gets back up again.

The last speech is finally, blessedly, over. If I ever get married myself, I'm definitely skipping the toasts. Then again, even if I wasn't a member of the Never a Bride club, the little bean I'm growing makes any fairy tale ending unlikely.

Jamie voices what we're all thinking when he asks loudly, "Cake now?"

The *three* wedding photographers (official wedding photographer, assistant to the official wedding photographer, and bridal magazine photographer) crowd around Ricky and Nicole as they go through the pantomime of cutting the first piece of that scrumptious cake. They feed it to each other playfully, Nicole looking like a million dollars worth of white gold, and Ricky grinning like a lunatic, frosting on his lips.

"They are revolting," Lani says, but even though her words are harsh, she's got a grudging smile on her face. She acts like a tough cookie, but I suspect she's got a marshmallowy center.

"Aw, I think they're cute. This wedding is the bomb!" This from Zack, another one of the groomsmen, a cute-blond-skater type who was Ricky's roommate freshman year. "Wanna get some cake?"

"Okay, sure," Lani says. She lets him pull her up out of her chair. I'm positive they hooked up after the rehearsal dinner last night. Lani is a mystery to me. Of all of us, she's the most, um, friendly with the opposite sex, but she's definitely the most strident anti-long-term relationship one, at least after Rosie and Ophelia promptly lost their Never a Bride credentials by falling in love with Gus and Jamie respectively over the past year.

Jamie and Ophelia, with their notorious penchant for sweets, have already abandoned us to be first in line for cake. Rosie and Gus are slow-dancing. I wrack my brain for something to say to the remaining groomsman, Jared, but all I can remember about him is he's a venture capitalist like Ricky. Since I tend to zone out when Ricky's talking about work I'm not exactly bursting with topical conversation.

Before I make some inane comment about the wedding, Oliver's unmistakable voice sounds at my ear. "May I join you?"

I look over my shoulder. He looks—God, he looks *good*. I wish I would stop noticing how handsome he is, how pretty and sleek and how much I want to muss him up like he was mussed the night we met. I tamp that impulse down as far as it will go. This is not the time or the place to indulge our unfortunate physical chemistry.

"Sure," I manage.

He takes Lani's empty seat. "Would you care for some cake?" he asks politely. "I'd be happy to get you some."

I'm genuinely speechless, until I remember that some men in their thirties actually have such a thing as social graces. It's just that as a lifelong resident of Los Angeles, I haven't met very many of them.

"That would be lovely, thank you," I say when I recover my voice.

He rises as elegantly as he sat down. "Be right back."

I watch him walk away, not sure what's happening. He doesn't seem particularly freaked out, the way I was after I found out I was going to be a mom. Maybe it's different for guys. He doesn't have an actual living thing growing inside him.

I glance over at Jared, but he's looking at his phone, so I

figure I'm off the hook, conversation-wise. Instead I wait for Oliver to come back with cake for me, as if I'm his date. As if we're together, and not what we are, one-night-stand-turned-co-parents. If that's even what he wants. God. I need to stop thinking. None of this is going to be resolved tonight, and I promised myself I would enjoy this wedding for Nicole's sake if nothing else.

So when Oliver returns, two plates of cake balanced carefully on one hand and forearm, carrying a steaming cup of coffee in the other, I do my best to act like a normal person. I was a professional actress. I can pull this off.

"Coffee?" he asks. "It's decaf."

Sweet of him to offer me something I can drink. "Thanks, but I'll probably only have a sip. Do you want it?"

"I'll have a sip, too. I'm a sucker for coffee and cake together."

"This cake is so amazing you might not need the coffee. I got an early preview a few months ago."

We take simultaneous bites of sugar-butter-flour and moan. I'm not super into dessert, but this is a damn good cake.

"Damn," he says, as if he can read my thoughts. "That's good."

"I know." We eat in companionable silence for a minute.

"I'm going to have to track down the person that made this little piece of heaven. My mom's coming to visit for her birthday and she'd go crazy for this."

"When's that?"

"End of July. She's arriving a few days after the restaurant opens."

"So that's here in Santa Barbara?"

"Mercy SB, right in the middle of the Funk Zone."

"And you said you have another location?"

"Two, actually." He scrapes frosting off his plate with the side of his fork, slides it into his mouth and out again, leaving a trace of buttercream on his upper lip. "One in West Hollywood. The original is in Eagle Rock."

"Wait. *Mercy*? The uber-hip restaurant where Ashton Kutcher goes all the time?"

He smiles with pride. "You've been there?"

"No." I vaguely remember it opening around the time Ben died and I've basically been a social hermit since then. The first year, I had an excuse. The last couple of years, not going out with my dwindling list of friends has been habit.

"I hope you'll come visit. Or at least be at the opening of the new one, since it's a bit closer to home for you."

"Closer?" I'm confused, until it dawns that he must think I live here in Santa Barbara. "Oh, I live in Los Feliz."

At that, he jerks his head up. "Really? I'm in Silver Lake."

In Los Angeles's sprawling quilt of mini-cities, that makes us practically neighbors. "But we went to that apartment..." For some reason bringing up that night makes me uncomfortable. Maybe it's easier to sit here talking over cake when I can pretend we haven't seen each other naked.

"That's my friend J.T.'s place. We were camping, and I came back early. He let me crash there."

"Oh, that makes so much more sense." I recall the vibe of the apartment, messy and frat-boyish, which doesn't line up at all with how Oliver strikes me now.

He grins at me. Again, it's as if he can read my thoughts. "I think we have a lot to learn about each other."

I'm about to point out that there's not much point in learning about each other given the extent of our relationship will hopefully boil down to a simple contract. But I bite my tongue. I'm supposed to be enjoying the wedding and fighting with Oliver isn't going to make it more fun.

Instead I try to stay light. "Well, the night is young. What do you want to know?"

He smiles and leans close, as if we're sharing a secret. "Only everything."

Oh shit.

I may be determined to make the best of this situation, but I'm not prepared for the intensity of his tone, or the look in his eyes, as if he truly wants to know everything about me.

I shiver. I need to be more careful what I wish for.

CHAPTER 11

OLIVER

"The way I see it, we have a unique opportunity to get to know each other." I speak slowly, distracted as I am by the way Kate's glossy lips wrap around her fork as she consumes her slice of truly excellent wedding cake. "Let's play a game."

She swallows, and I pretend I don't want to lick the trace of frosting off the corner of her mouth. I'm trying to prove to her I'm responsible father material, not trying to seduce her.

She pushes away her empty plate and squints. "A game? Like poker?"

"No, like Truth or Dare. Or Never Have I Ever."

"A drinking game?" She sighs with feeling. "I can't drink, more's the pity."

I forgot for a second she's pregnant and therefore not drinking. Not to mention the last time we drank together we ended up in bed, and that's definitely not the point of this exercise.

"Right, Truth or Dare it is. But you can only pick Dare once. Everything else you have to answer."

"Harsh terms." She sounds intrigued.

"But efficient." It's not the most organic way to get to know someone, but we're on the clock.

"Okay. It'll be like speed dating," she says, then her cheeks color petal-pink. "Except, you know, not the dating part."

I nod, relieved we're on the same page. "Exactly." This is merely a get-to-know-you exercise, a chance for me to show her that I'm more complex than at first glance. Sort of like the wedding cake. I've got layers.

But for this to work, we need more privacy. Her tablemates are wandering back and I don't want her censored by having an audience. I jump up and grab her hand, intending to lead her to some secluded corner, but taking off altogether would be even better. "You want to get out of here?" I ask hopefully.

She scrunches up her face. "Bridesmaid. I think Nicole would kill me if I disappeared."

"Well, we can't have that." I don't want to give Nicole or Ricky any reason to be put out with me. Does knocking up one of their best friends qualify? Before I can come up with Plan B, one of the bridesmaids, the one in the mermaid dress, shuffles up to us, a fake-looking smile on her face.

"Going somewhere?" she asks.

"Nowhere," Kate says quickly. "Rosie, this is—" If I wasn't watching her carefully, I might not have noticed the slight thinning of her lips as she works through how to introduce me. "Oliver."

"Oliver Mercier." I flash Rosie my most ingratiating smile, but it doesn't do much to alleviate her suspicion that I'm trying to spirit away her friend. "So nice to meet you, Rosie. Nicole has the most ravishing bridesmaids I've ever seen."

I may have overdone it, because she just scowls harder.

"How do you know Kate?" she asks pointedly.

I glance at the woman whose hand I'm still holding. She's frozen, looking at me, eyes wide. Maybe she doesn't want to out me without my permission. Maybe Rosie doesn't know she's pregnant. Or no—Rosie's the doctor friend, right? The one who figured out she was pregnant in the first place.

I stick with the truth, or part of it. "Ricky's working with me on a business venture and he was gracious enough to include me tonight."

"That's right. Oliver's a restaurateur. He's opening a new place in the Funk Zone."

"Oh. That's so interesting," Rosie says in a voice that says she thinks that's about as interesting as learning I have a sexually transmitted disease.

Kate shoots her a look that probably means something in girl language. "We were just going to take a little walk."

"I'll come with you," Rosie says immediately.

"Um, can I talk to you?" Kate says to Rosie. She pulls her hand away from mine so she can herd Rosie to the other side of the table where they talk in hushed tones. I feign interest in the centerpiece, an ornate arrangement of fresh flowers in different shades of green and white. I sneak a glance at the two women. Rosie is frowning, but at Kate, not at me, so maybe that's progress.

"I'll be back in a little while," I hear Kate say.

"Nice to meet you," I call back to Rosie. I take Kate's arm, leading her toward the pool. Her bare feet glow white against the dark lawn beneath us. "Should we get you some shoes?"

"My flats are in the coatroom."

I switch direction and steer us toward the main building. I don't let go of Kate and she lets me hold on. She feels warm and delicate tucked under my arm, like an apricot blossom in the spring sunshine.

"So does she hate me?"

Kate seems to know I'm talking about Rosie. "She's just surprised. I'd been having a little bit of trouble tracking you down. I think she was ready to believe I'd made you up."

"Immaculate conception?"

"Honestly, to the bridesmaids that almost makes more sense than what really happened."

"So, you really don't...hook up...that often?"

"Are we playing already?"

"Playing?"

"Truth or One Dare?"

I'd almost forgotten my proposal to speed up the getting to know each other process. "Oh yeah. Yes."

"Then, no, I never hook up."

"So why me?" I cringe after the words come out of my mouth. If I'm trying to get her to see my non-self-absorbed side, so far I'm doing a stellar job.

She stumbles and I tighten my grip. Instead of answering she says, "Isn't it my turn?"

"Okay, go ahead."

"Are you financially solvent?"

"You can ask me anything and you want to know about my finances?"

"It's relevant to our situation, don't you think?"

She's got a point, and she's got balls. Where I come from, talking about money is as verboten as talking about politics and religion.

"I'm a restaurateur. My business entity carries some debt, but I'm not personally exposed. My finances are fine. I own my place in Silver Lake, with a manageable mortgage, and I have a decent savings cushion thanks to wise management of my trust fund. I don't spend more than I make and I don't cheat on my taxes. Okay?"

That seems to appease her, though I won't be surprised if she asks to see my tax returns. Nothing wrong with transparency. I make a mental note to have Nat email them to Kate on Monday.

Oh God. Nat. She's going to laugh so hard when she finds out about this.

"Thanks. That's reassuring."

"What about you? Are you a broke millennial?"

She laughs. "Well, I'm pretty careful with my money. I rent my apartment. I've driven the same car for years. But I make good money at my job, and I still get residuals from when I was acting. I've already run the numbers and I'll be able to support this baby even if you don't want to contribute."

I forget that she's had a couple of extra weeks to get used to the idea. I admire her practicality, but for some reason I don't want her to be thinking of this as a purely transactional relationship. She's all business, while I still want to lick that frosting off her lip.

We stop by the coatroom and she grabs some flat shoes and a pashmina out of a tote bag. There's a bench in the hallway where she sits to put them on.

"It's your turn," I prompt, feeling the urgency to keep the game going. If we don't, maybe we'll lose this sense of intimacy.

"Tell me about your family. Are you close with them?"

"Sort of. My father is French, but he's lived in the States since he was a young man. He owns a wine import business based in New York City. That's where I was born. He met my mom on a wine-buying trip to Paris in the early '80s and brought her home with him. She's French Moroccan. Used to be a well-known model. Now she helps Papa and does her own thing, charities and stuff. I have a younger brother—married with twin boys. He works with Papa. And that's basically it. I'm the black sheep. I avoided the wine business but couldn't help getting into an even less secure industry. It turns out I've had success so far."

"What's your mom's name?"

"Aziza Amine."

"Your mom is *Aziza*? The supermodel?"

I laugh. I always forget how famous she was once upon a time.

"Yeah."

"Holy shit." She side-eyes me. "No wonder you're so pretty."

It's nothing I haven't heard before. "Why do you think I grew the beard?"

She turns more fully toward me. "It suits you." She raises a hand, looks almost like she's going to touch my face, then drops it back to her lap. "Even if it covers up your dimple."

I feel...strange. I'm used to coasting on my good looks, and I'm as vain as the next guy, which is pretty vain, honestly. But Kate's quiet appraisal makes me feel light and warm all over.

There's something about her, how composed she is, that makes me want to be someone she can be proud of. At the same time, I want to find a way under her skin. If I cracked her cool exterior, what would she be like when she's not so tightly in control?

That's the Kate I remember from the night we spent together, someone a little wild, a little fast, free with her kisses. The Kate whose hair was down and who arched up into me when I bunched my fist in those long red locks and pulled.

I clear my throat, willing away those erotic images, and ignore my chubbing-up cock.

"My turn," I murmur. She must hear something in my voice because she inches away. Probably for the best. "Why don't you date?"

She takes a deep breath. "It's complicated."

I wait. Mercier men can draw on a deep well of patience if the reward is great enough.

"I don't date because I don't want to."

"That's complicated?"

"Well, I guess boiled down it's not that complicated, but I —" She bites her lip and I haven't seen her this twisted up since she was trying to get it through my thick skull that she was pregnant with our baby. "You'll find out sometime, so I might as well tell you."

"Find what out?" I ask, praying this isn't communicable disease related. If we weren't careful enough not to get pregnant, we sure as hell weren't careful enough to not share anything else one of us might have. I'm ninety-nine percent certain I'm clean. I better suggest we both get tested at the doctor's visit we'll have to schedule for the paternity test anyway. Not that I don't trust her, but Nat will insist.

"I was engaged a few years ago. To my college boyfriend. Ben."

Things become clearer. He must have hurt her badly. "Messy breakup?"

"No. He died."

"Shit."

I don't realize I've said that out loud until she nods, sadly. "Yeah, it was extremely shitty."

"What happened?"

"A couple of months before the wedding he got hit by a car riding his bike home. On Vermont, you know that intersection near the 101?" She doesn't wait for me to respond. "And he died, and I haven't dated since."

"When did it happen?"

"About three years ago."

"Fuck. Kate, I'm so sorry."

"Yeah, me too. I froze for a while. I'd been cast in a network drama and I couldn't go through with it. I quit acting, lived off my savings until a friend roped me into producing his podcast, and it turned out I was good at it. I'm more comfortable behind the scenes now. That's it. That's why I don't date."

I'm puzzled. I get that she'd been in mourning. But to entirely close up shop seems a bit extreme. I'm about to press her a little on that, but she beats me to it.

"My turn. I have to ask you something I've been wondering about. Why are you not freaking the fuck out right now?"

"What do you mean?"

"I mean out of the blue some random chick you slept with told you she's having your baby and you've been nothing but chill. Please tell me this is the first time this has happened to you. I mean, you don't have any other kids, right?"

I chuckle. "I don't have any other kids. And I don't quite know why I'm not freaking out. I probably will later. Maybe it's a delayed effect. But there's just something, I don't know. I always thought I'd have a kid someday. And my parents taught me to take responsibility for my actions, so what else am I going to do? Have a tantrum and rail at the world that this wasn't in my plans? I'm single, I'm thirty-five, I'm financially secure, as we already established. Maybe this is the way it was always supposed to happen. Don't you believe in signs?"

"Knocking someone up isn't a sign. It's a big fat mistake you can't take back." Her words are caustic, but her tone isn't.

"Is that how you feel? That this is a mistake? You don't have to go through with it, you know. It's not too late for an abortion, or if you don't want to actually raise the kid, I can do it on my own. But I'm not going to send you a check every month and then disappear. I can't. And I don't want to."

She's silent for so long I wonder if I've gone too far. I know in the big scheme of things what I want isn't the most important thing, but I have to be honest. Truth or Dare rules.

When she finally speaks the bitterness in her voice shocks me. "You really want to raise a kid with me, a girl you barely know, who's so frigid and so fucked up from losing someone that she can't handle it when a nice, cute guy asks her to dinner?"

Frigid? Fucked up? Are we talking about the same amazing, undeniably hot woman?

"I don't remember asking you to dinner."

"No, someone else, if you can believe it."

"Kate, I'd believe it if you told me you got asked out every goddamned day. And to answer your question, yes, I do want to raise a kid with you. Will it be crazy and a huge learning curve and stressful sometimes? Probably. I didn't know anything about the restaurant business when I started and I caught on fast. I can do this, too."

"You're either really confident, or really stupid."

"Look, how bad can it be?"

She laughs, looks sad. "Pretty fucking bad, actually."

"You told me you were happy about the baby. Was that a lie?"

"No. I want to be a mom."

She doesn't sound equivocal about that at least.

"So it's me you aren't sure about. I get that. You barely know me from Adam." My heart rate picks up, worried that everything I've done to try to convince her to give me a chance has been for nothing. I pick up her hand gently, cradling it in mine. Her posture is stiff—I've never seen her with anything less than steel in her backbone—but her hand is soft. "But I'm going to do my best to be there for you and for this baby. Can you let me do that?"

"Are we still playing the game?"

I freeze. I don't want to play games with her. I want...with a start, I realize that I want *her*. I mean, yeah, I've wanted her with a sort of low-level urge ever since I saw her walking down the aisle in her ridiculous dress. I remember the night we spent together and how perfect her legs were wrapped around me, and how her hair felt bunched up in my hands, piles of it spread out on the pillows. But that was the simplistic desire of a man for a beautiful woman. I want *Kate*. I want her bossiness and her insecurity and her laugh and I want to hold her hand and I want to lick the shell of her ear and between her breasts and catalog how those tastes are different and how they're the same.

I open my mouth, incapable of telling her, not when we're balancing on a precipice and she could push me off at any moment. My voice is serious when I finally get out, "I don't think we're playing games here, Kate."

"No, we're not. But I need a timeout just the same." She pulls her hand away from me, gets up, and walks away.

CHAPTER 12

KATE

R unning away from Oliver is about the most cowardly thing I can do, but I can't help it. It was the hand-holding thing, honestly. And the fact that Oliver's taking his impending fatherhood a hell of a lot better than I expected, or earned.

I run back to the middle of the party, feeling mildly guilty for disappearing for so long. Nicole and Ricky are center stage on the dance floor as the band plays disco. They seem to be having the time of their lives. They deserve the best night ever.

A stab of rage slams into my gut. It takes me a second to place the target of my anger—myself. If I were a normal person with an IUD like every other sexually active woman my age, my night would be going much differently. I'd be dancing with Oliver, maybe planning a repeat of our previous activities. Not planning to raise a kid together. If I were a normal person, someone holding my hand wouldn't send tingles right to my core.

I really need to get my mind off sex—specifically sex with Oliver.

I skim my eyes over the crowd. Lani's dancing with someone I don't recognize. Ophelia and Jamie are making eyes at each other over a plate of macarons. Where did those come from? I don't see Rosie or Gus, but I feel a tug on my arm and Rosie hisses in my ear, "We need to talk."

I sigh. Rosie's mother hen schtick is getting old. "I'm fine. I told you before."

"You've been gone forever. What did he say? Is he nice? Do I need to break his arm?"

I lift my eyebrows at my friend. "Aren't doctors supposed to do no harm?"

"Gus didn't take the Hippocratic oath. He can do it."

"Gus wouldn't hurt a fly. Besides, no arms need breaking. Oliver's actually been really cool about the whole thing." I sigh again. I should be happy that he's making this easy on me, but honestly I'm finding the entire night emotionally exhausting. It would have been easier if he'd blown up, refused to believe me or to have anything to do with me. Then I could have written him off guilt-free and I wouldn't have to deal with all these pesky feelings.

"Really? What did he say? What's he like?"

I cast about for a way to characterize the father of my child. "He's...a grownup," I say wryly, "despite his apparent habit of picking up girls in nightclubs. He's got his own business and a savings account. Oh, his mom is an '80s supermodel."

Rosie is patently unimpressed. "That's all great, but what did he say about the baby?"

"He wants to be involved. I gave him an out—many of them —and he refuses to take one."

She frowns. "And how do you feel about that?"

Horrifyingly, I feel tears well up in my eyes.

"Oh, honey, here." Rosie, ever prepared, has tissues at the ready. I take one and dab my eyes.

"At first, I just wanted him to be okay with stepping aside, letting me do it all. Then I wouldn't have to negotiate or compromise." Rosie smiles slightly. "Yes, I know those aren't my favorite things. But, if he means what he says, I can't deny him a chance to be a dad. And I don't want to. It'll be better for the little jelly bean, in any case." I twist the tissue into a knot. "So I'll do my best to get over my control issues and we'll try to do this together. But, Rosie, that's not what has me turned around. I'm…I haven't felt like this in a long time. A really long time."

"Felt like what?"

"Like…I like him."

"Oh." Rosie doesn't seem to know how to respond to that.

"And what if that feeling doesn't go away? What if I keep liking him?"

"Would that be so bad? To like your kid's dad?"

"Yes! That would be terrible! It would be just like in *Sex and the City* when Miranda's in love with Steve and he's got that new girlfriend and they co-parent with her pining after him for, like, a year."

"Yeah, but don't Steve and Miranda end up together?"

"That's not the point. What if I'm pining away for Oliver and he's parading around this string of girls? I get the impression that he's not exactly into monogamy. Or commitment."

"Last I checked, neither are you. Or have you forgotten the whole Never a Bride thing?"

"You should talk! You're cohabitating, for fuck's sake."

"This isn't about me," Rosie says calmly. Damn her. "What happened to 'I'm never getting married, I don't date, blah blah blah?'"

"Grow up, Rosie, I said that stuff because my fiancé died and I was scared to let myself love again!" My voice has risen, but luckily the band drowns me out.

"Wow. I knew that. I just didn't know *you* knew it." Rosie looks proud of me for being as self-aware as I am. I make a mental note to tell my therapist the thousands of dollars I've spent on her haven't been entirely wasted.

"You're afraid if you like this guy, he's not going to like you back and that's going to make things difficult?"

"I'm afraid of a lot of things," I concede. "But definitely the scariest thing at the moment is that I'm kind of into him. The baby stuff—that's all theoretical. I mean I'm sure eventually the baby will feel more real, but right now that's all in the future. What's right here and now is Oliver, and he's being so sweet and holding my hand and—"

"He held your hand?"

"Yeah, and he's wearing the hell out of his suit and that night we spent together I was pretty drunk, but it was still amazing, and all I can think about is what it would be like if we did it sober and I blame all these fucking hormones and the wedding and the fact that I'm severely undersexed—I mean, I've had sex once in three years. That's not enough, Rosie. You know. You and Gus probably do it every night."

She blushes. "Not *every* night."

I mentally applaud Gus's stamina. "What am I going to do?" I finish my pathetic little freak-out and look at her hopefully, as if she'll come to my rescue yet again.

"If you like him, you could ask him if he likes you, too."

"I was a one-night stand."

"Did he tell you that? I mean, how did you leave it with him that night?"

"I sort of, um, snuck out before he woke up."

Rosie does her best not to laugh right in my face. "And tonight, when you ran into each other at the wedding, how did he act? Was he avoiding you?"

I think back to our encounter in the coatroom. He'd sought me out. He'd wanted a dance. Maybe more.

I relent. "Okay, so maybe he doesn't find me repulsive. But won't sleeping together again make things more confusing?"

"I don't know, sweetie. But I think you owe it to yourself to find out if there's something there. You've been isolating your-self for too long. I say, go for it."

"Really?"

"I survived being a bridesmaid once, I could do it again." She squeezes my arm reassuringly. "And if it doesn't go well, then I'll be there, too."

I smile at her, so grateful we've gotten closer over this last year of wedding planning. "I know you will. Thanks."

I take a shaky breath. Admitting you have a problem is the first step, right? I can't believe I'm considering embarking on a physical relationship with someone I barely know. There are so many possible terrible outcomes. There's no way this choose-your-own adventure can end any way but badly.

Rosie reads the ambivalence on my face. "You can do this. You're so brave, Kate."

Brave? For so long, being brave meant forcing myself out of bed every morning. It meant starting my podcast production company. It meant going through the wedding planning nonsense with a sometimes tone-deaf Nicole. But now I under-stand that wasn't really being brave. That was survival.

Maybe now I'm ready to do more than just survive. Am I strong enough, brave enough, to go after something I really want? Something that would mean I'd be more than surviving?

I'd be living again.

I hug Rosie, grab my purse, and head to the bathroom. I wash my hands, examine my face in the mirror. My makeup was under-stated to start with—Nicole wanted us to look like "flowers after a spring rain" in our poppy-colored dresses. I touch up my blush and lipstick, smooth down the wisps of hair that have escaped my bun. What the hell—I pull the bun out entirely. I'd worn my hair down the night of the bachelorette. Maybe Oliver likes long hair.

I've had plenty of practice accentuating my attributes to get things I want. Being a successful actress is often about being in the right place at the right time, and definitely about being prepared, reliable, and a team player. But having a killer body, attractive face, and masses of soft, naturally red hair don't hurt, either.

If I were pulling out all the stops, I'd switch my comfy flats back for those fucking heels, but I'm not that much of a masochist. Instead, I adjust my pushup bra and admire the consequent hint of décolletage.

Showtime.

CHAPTER 13

KATE

Of course, best laid plans. I can't find Oliver anywhere. Instead, the band has vanished and the DJ Nicole hired for the last phase of the wedding festivities has taken over, playing contemporary dance music that has the oldsters retiring to their seats. The youngsters take their place, loose and goofy and slightly buzzed. It looks like fun and I suddenly want to join them. There's nothing like dancing to make me forget about my problems and just feel free.

That's what happened the night of the bachelorette. While the other girls were busy making sure Nicole was having fun and staying hydrated, I was happy for an excuse to cut loose and dance, not caring about how I looked or how I felt. I hadn't done that in ages. Ben was an enthusiastic dancer, not especially coordinated, but he didn't give a shit. He'd twirl me around, do the robot, give it his all. He knew I loved dancing and he loved me, so...

Just like that, my mood sours into a clutch of regret. I'm sad, yes, but I'm also angry that three years later I still have trouble enjoying something I love because it reminds me of what I've lost. I back away from the crowd, heart thundering, dizzy with emotional whiplash.

I bump into a body and whirl around, apology on my lips. It's Ricky. "Sorry."

"You coming out on the dance floor?" He smiles at me wide and guileless, his cheeks red from exertion and exhilaration.

Impulsively, I give him a hug. He freezes, and I can't blame him. I've known him for at least a decade, but we've never been super close. We don't hang out if Nicole's not there, and I've always tolerated the stodgy, capitalist, enlight-ened-frat-boy thing he has going on. He pats my back awkwardly. I pull away with a jerk when I become aware of what I'm doing.

But he's still smiling, looks pleased, even, when I check out his expression. "What was that for?"

"I'm just really, really happy for you guys," I whisper, my throat full. "You have the best girl. You know that, right?"

"I know." He worships Nicole, always has. She expects no less. But he also tempers her, challenges her. She wouldn't have gone to Parsons if he hadn't encouraged her, hadn't dragged her out of her comfortable SoCal bubble and taken her away to New York for all those years. They grew up there, and when they came home, Nicole to set up her own design business and Ricky to make a living investing in other people's visions, they were different. They were legit.

Back then, I felt more like a child than ever, lost and still in a fog from losing Ben. They were there for me, never demand-ing, always including me as much as I deigned to be included. Nicole came down every other week to take me to lunch. Ricky introduced me to acquaintances who turned into clients. They've been extraordinary friends. I'm ashamed to realize I've never said thank you.

Before I get a word out, Ricky says, "I have to tell you how much I appreciate everything you've done to get us here. Nicole's been intense about the wedding, to say the least. But you've never complained. I know she's having the night of her life tonight because of all the hard work you and the other girls put in."

I'm about to shrug it all off, part and parcel of being friends with Nicole, even though his words do make me feel warm inside. But he goes on, voice softer. "I know it couldn't have been easy to take all this on. Ben would have been really proud of how strong you've been. You're incredible, Kate."

My breath catches on hearing his name coming from someone else's lips. My friends don't exactly talk about him all the time, probably because they don't want to bring up any memories. It wouldn't matter, since he's on my mind all the time anyway. But to hear Ricky mention him, it means a lot. I forget sometimes that they were good friends. We were all at school together, went on plenty of double dates back in the day. Ben convinced Ricky of the importance of investing in companies with a social conscience, of using investment money to spur change in established companies. He'd even asked Ricky to be a groomsman at our wedding. Ricky and Nicole ended up flying out for a funeral instead of a wedding.

But I have no idea if Ben would be proud of me. Not right now. Pregnant with a stranger's kid? Unable to do something as simple as allowing myself to dance? Unable to simply forget about him for five seconds in order to figure out what I want?

Ricky's waiting for me to say something, anything. I blow out a hot breath instead of bursting into tears, because poor Ricky doesn't deserve that. "I don't know about that. I know I seem strong, but it's like my shell is calcified, holding me up, but inside I'm broken."

His smile vanishes and his eyes widen. Then he puts his arms around me. "Ben was always proud of you. He couldn't believe you picked him. You made him really happy."

I couldn't stop the tears if I tried. I sniffle into Ricky's shoulder.

"You don't have to hear it from me to know that he'd want

you to be happy. You know that he would want everything for you, even if he couldn't be the one to give it to you."

I'd never thought about it that way before. I'd always thought about it in more basic terms, that Ben wouldn't have wanted me to give up, to succumb to grief, to let myself die a little bit more every day without him. So I didn't. But I'd been dragging my feet on all the rest and now it's all happening so fast, I'm wobbly. But Ricky's right. Ben wouldn't want me to have half a life. He'd want me to have it all, everything we would have had together. For the first time in a long time, I want it all, too.

Ricky produces a handkerchief for my tears and I wipe my previously beautiful face, lamenting all the time I spent fixing it up in the bathroom. Oh well.

I give Ricky one more squeeze, then let him go. "You know, I think Nicole just might have the best guy, too."

He looks down at his feet. "Thanks, Kate."

"You better go dance some more."

"You coming?"

"In a minute, promise." I smile, trying to feel it. He nods and leaves me, and I feel bad for every time I ever rolled my eyes behind his back at his Boy Scout sensibilities. There are so many worse things than a good guy who loves his wife. Even if he does wear his polo shirt collar popped sometimes.

CHAPTER 14

OLIVER

After Kate abandons me outside the coatroom, I sit for a while, uncertain what my next move should be. It's getting late, and even though the reception seems far from over, I'm not sure what else I can accomplish tonight. It's already been the most eventful wedding I've ever attended, and the bouquet hasn't even been thrown. Since I'm not about to get drunk or find someone to take back to my hotel room, my options are limited.

Is this what life is going to be like now? I'm not a huge partier, but I don't exactly put limits on my alcohol consumption unless I have a morning meeting. Women are a different story. I don't have someone new in my bed every week, exactly, but let's just say that I've never gone stag to a wedding and failed to find someone to keep me company by night's end.

The idea of picking someone up seems ludicrous now. The only person I want to come home with me tonight is Kate, and that's tricky for a whole host of reasons.

My best play is going to my hotel and getting some sleep. Perhaps my acute awareness of everything Kate-related will fade in the light of day, once all of this sinks in.

I heave to my feet, trying to remember the way back to

where I relinquished my car a lifetime ago. But I can't leave without saying goodbye to Kate, even if she doesn't want to see me right now. She has my cell, but I don't have hers. It feels like she could disappear all too easily, just as she did that night we first met. I remember all too well the sense of disappointment, even hurt, I felt when I woke up alone in J.T.'s bed. I'd promised her pancakes; she'd promised to stay. She didn't even leave a note.

Back on the dance floor, the crowd is gyrating to a Lady Gaga remix. I don't see Kate anywhere in the crush of people. She's not at her table, either, or at any of the other tables. I spot a flash of poppy orange but it's the maid of honor, a head shorter than Kate. Damn.

"Ricky!" With relief, I snag the groom himself, who's getting a glass of something amber from the bar. "Have you seen Kate?"

"Yeah, man, I just saw her. Why?" He eyes me with suspicion. "Everything okay?"

My unease must be showing on my face and I try to school myself. "Of course, yeah. Fine. I just want—" *Everything.* I still want everything. "—to see if she wants to dance."

That doesn't seem to appease him. He narrows his eyes at me, as if he can peer into my soul and deduce my intentions. I scrape together my nerves and my dignity, hoping I pass inspection.

"Well, she said she'd get out on the dance floor, but I think she needed a minute."

"Sure." My shoulders sag as my irrational fear eases. She hasn't left. I don't want to leave without seeing her again. Without saying goodbye. Without promising her that this is all going to be okay. That I'm not going to let her down.

"How do you know Kate, anyway?"

"Uh, you introduced us." How could he possibly keep track of all the interactions he's had tonight?

"I don't think so," he says, voice eerily level. "Try again."

Fuck. I feel like I'm staring into the barrel of an overprotective brother's shotgun.

"We met on State Street a couple of months ago." That apparently means something to him, because his eyes widen a fraction. He steps into my personal space and I shift back infinitesimally.

"Couple of months ago, huh? And you just ran into her tonight? And now you want to dance with her?"

"Um. Yes?" I have no idea if Ricky knows what's going on with Kate, but it's clear he knows something, because he's giving me the protective vibe like whoa.

"Kate's like my sister."

I find myself nodding uncontrollably.

"And if you do anything, and I mean anything, to hurt her in any way, I won't just destroy your business and you personally, I will destroy anyone who does business with you."

"Jesus, man, relax." Trying to get Ricky to chill has the opposite of the intended effect. He looms closer.

"I mean it."

"I get it. Message received." I hold my ground, willing myself not to flinch.

"Good." He leans back and I let out a breath. "Enjoy the party."

I scrub a hand over my face as he walks away. I'm glad that Kate has friends in her corner, but I'm a bit outnumbered here. Not to mention that Ricky might actually be able to ruin me if he set his mind to it. I don't need an incentive not to hurt Kate, but I'm still a little wobbly when I resume my search for her.

Finally, I find her hovering on the edge of the dance floor, watching the dancers but not moving much herself. She looks young, lovely, and sad.

I'm hit with a wave of self-doubt. What right do I have to offer her anything at all? It's not as if my track record at nurturing relationships has been all that wonderful. The longest relationships I've had with women have been decidedly nonsexual in nature. Kate and I have a much better chance of making this work if we stay completely platonic from here on out.

Then I register she's let her hair out of its bun and it's falling in waves over her shoulders. I remember that hair sweeping over my chest, sliding like silk through my fingers, piled decadently on my pillow. Who am I kidding? I'm not an idiot. I know it's a bad idea to fuck around with the future mother of one's child. It would be messy and foolish and I pride myself on being fastidious and smart.

So why do I want to go to her, shove my fingers into her hair, and kiss her senseless?

The music changes to something with a heavy bass line, thumping and insistent, echoing the rhythm of my heart. Kate notes the change, starts shifting her hips in time to the music, and I watch, unable to tear my gaze away. Ten times lovelier than anyone else on the dance floor, she takes a couple of steps forward, brings her arms up, lets go of her hesitation. I recognize the song, something we danced to together months ago. I didn't realize it until now, but I haven't forgotten anything about that night. I thought I'd lost my redheaded siren, and here I am, having been given the most incredible second chance.

I slip off my jacket, sling it over the back of a chair, fumble with the buttons on my cuffs, roll up my sleeves. Time to go to work.

I press through the crowd, easing as close to Kate's side as I can get without touching her. She's already deep into the groove, but it takes me a second to find the beat of the song. She acknowledges me with a tip of her head and doesn't move away. I'm beginning to get to know her so I know that says a lot. She's allowing me access and I'm grateful for it. I won't push for more.

We dance like that, not touching, virtually synched up.

Song after song, my world consists of the dance floor under our feet, the music in our ears, and the woman swaying and turning at my side. Eventually I loosen my tie, undo the top buttons of the dress shirt I'm doing my best not to sweat through. Kate's eyelids drop as her gaze latches onto the V of skin I've exposed. In silent retaliation she twists her hair into a mass on top of her head with one hand, fans her elegant swan's neck with the other. We're both out of breath but neither of us makes a move to stop.

We don't touch but I can feel her nonetheless. Is it possible to be this bound up with someone this quickly? This night has taken on a surreal quality, the magic of the twinkling lights, the sweeping fabric of the tents, the thump of the music, the tinkle of laughter. We're all here to celebrate something practically mundane—people get married every day, just as relationships fall apart every day—but this feels different. There's real love here. Love between Ricky and Nicole, between Kate and her friends. Not to mention I know I'm going to love the little being that Kate's fearlessly, impossibly, growing.

I'm closer to being in love with Kate than any woman I've ever met.

That alone should make my blood run cold, should make me turn and run, should make me retreat back into my easy, carefree bachelor existence. But maybe I've been tired of all that for a while. Maybe I've been looking for a way to move on. Maybe this is my chance.

Over Kate's shoulder, I spot the blonde bridesmaid asleep with her head on a table. Nearby, Nicole and Ricky say their goodbyes and press neatly boxed leftover cake into the hands of their departing guests. They must be exhausted.

I glance at Kate. I wonder when she got up this morning, how busy her day before the wedding was. How is she not dead on her feet? There's no way she's driving back to Los Feliz tonight.

I touch her elbow and she jerks as if I've electrocuted her.

"Sorry." I raise my voice to be heard over the music. "Where are you staying?"

She bites her lip. "Nicole and Ricky's house. They're staying here tonight and leaving for their honeymoon in the morning. I'm housesitting for a couple of days."

"Where's that? Can I drive you?"

"In the hills. I have a car."

It takes every ounce of my willpower not to immediately grow impatient at her stubborn display of independence and demand that she let me drive her. Instead, I breathe. Long game, I remind myself.

Then she surprises me for about the hundredth time tonight.

"But the party's not over," she says with a mischievous smile.

"I guess it's not."

We keep dancing.

CHAPTER 15

KATE

I t's been a vomit-inducing roller coaster of a night, but right now, dancing with Oliver, I feel like I'm flying.

He's matched me song for song, and his hair has fallen out of its pristine wave and over his forehead. His tie hangs loose and I want to grab him by it, pull him against my body, feel exactly how hot he is through his sweat-damp shirt. I know I must be sweaty, too, but I'm wearing comparatively much less clothing and I'm not really feeling it.

My face is probably red, my deodorant's long since worn off, and my makeup is a thing of the past. I may be a mess, but Oliver doesn't seem to care. In fact, he's stuck to me like glue, except, you know, literally. He hasn't touched me, except when he asked where I'm staying tonight. As if that's relevant to him.

I have no idea what he's thinking or what we're doing, I only know I don't want to stop dancing. I don't want to stop feeling this free. When I stop I'll have to think about the future. I'll have to think about what I want and accept it when I don't get it. But not yet. Not until I stop dancing. So I won't.

The DJ takes pity on us, shifts to something slower but still with a solid beat. I take a huge gulp of air, wish for a water bottle right about now. I twist around. Oliver looks absolutely delicious disheveled. He's a sexy dancer, for lack of a better word. He moves with a natural grace that speaks to him knowing how to move in other arenas. And I don't mean sports.

To prevent myself from plastering my body to him I say, "Water?"

He gets the message, disappears briefly, and returns to offer me a glass of cold water that I drain gratefully.

I'm vaguely aware that the night is winding down. Poor Ophelia's passed out at a table, but I trust Jamie to get her home. I haven't seen Lani or her skater-groomsman in ages, so I have a feeling they already took off for their own personal after-party. I don't see Rosie or Gus, or the other groomsmen, but everyone who doesn't live locally is staying at a hotel down the road, and I'm not in charge of them, thankfully.

In fact, since the wedding itself is officially over and the curtain is coming down on the reception, I'm off the clock. No more bridesmaid duties. No more planning. No more moral support. No more opinions. No more pretending to care about colors or flavors or fonts or the guest list or the seating chart.

I'm not a bridesmaid anymore.

My life is my own again. I'm free.

I glance down at my dress. Suddenly, I need it gone. I need to be rid of the binding corset and the color that clashes with my hair no matter what anybody else says.

I put my hands to my throat. Even though nothing covers it, I almost feel as if I'm suffocating. I have a change of clothes, but —shit—I've been sewn into the dress. I can't get out of it without help. I was going to ask Rosie, but the one time I actually need her tonight and she's nowhere to be found.

But Oliver's here.

"Oliver?"

"Yes, Kate?"

"Don't take this the wrong way, but can you help me take my dress off?"

He blinks at me once. Twice.

"Absolutely."

* * *

"We've got to stop meeting here," Oliver jokes when we're back in the coatroom for the third time tonight. I retrieve my larger bag, a wheeled one that holds the clothes I was wearing before I changed into my wedding costume, and myriad other things. I've got another bag in my car for my extended stay in Santa Barbara, but I can't wait to get to Ricky and Nicole's to get out of this dress.

But where to do it? People have been walking in and out of here all night—I need a place to change, but I don't have the key to the suite where the bride and groom are spending the night, even if I wanted to disturb it. Oliver can't come into the women's room in the lobby, but then I remember there's a large single bathroom down the hall.

"Come on." I head for it, knowing Oliver will follow. The bathroom's unoccupied and plenty roomy enough for what we need to do. Change clothes, I remind myself. Just change clothes. Nothing else.

Still, the atmosphere in here feels tense as I click the lock on the door and unzip the outer pocket of my bag to remove my sewing kit, including a seam ripper and a pair of scissors should it come to that. I avoid looking at Oliver, which is silly. We've been alone on and off all night, but not like this. Not with a locked door between us and the rest of the world.

"This dress is really something else," Oliver says.

I appreciate the distraction of his conversational foray.

"Nicole had each one designed specifically for us. We had to go to three fittings. She nearly had a heart attack when I told her I needed it to be let out three weeks ago."

"Let out?"

"Um, because my shape's already changing."

"Really?" He sounds almost excited. "Wow."

"Yeah." I laugh, a little shakily. "Anyway, the point is this dress is custom and even though I'm probably never going to wear it again, I don't want to destroy it. Do you know how to use this?" I hold up the seam ripper.

"Will I lose my masculine credibility with you if I say that I do?"

I roll my eyes. "No, I'll be impressed."

"In that case, yes. My mom's a fashion icon and didn't have daughters." He takes the small pronged tool. "Where do I rip?"

"There are two spots. One at the base of the bodice." I gesture behind me. "One under my arm. I could probably get the one under my arm, but I can't reach the back one. Start there."

Oliver moves behind me, stops. "Just to be clear, you want me to literally rip your bodice open? I thought bodice rippers were passé." His voice is amused.

I let out a startled laugh at the reference. "They are," I say firmly. "This is a special occasion. It's not like you're tearing it open with your bare hands or anything."

"Unfortunately." He mutters the word under his breath almost too low for me to catch. But not quite.

"Just do it. I'm dying to get out of this thing."

"Okay, okay." He leans over me. I crane my neck over my shoulder, but I can't see what he's doing.

"Do you see the seam?"

"I think so." He sounds like he's concentrating, then he puts a hand on my hip, to steady himself, I suppose, though the touch makes me feel jumpy and nervous. "Hold still."

"I am," I say, and force myself to stop moving. There's the impression of his fingers sliding against the fabric, gentle and patient. It triggers the sense memory of his fingers gliding across my skin, just as gentle, in complete control.

That night, it had been a relief to give myself over to someone who needed no direction, who had mastered the art of sex with strangers. The orgasms had exploded out of me. I hadn't been prepared for the force, or the quantity, of them. At the time I'd chalked up my response to the severe drought I'd imposed on myself, but now, with those same hands on my body, even through a layer of couture, I'm not sure it didn't have a bit to do with Oliver himself. The seeming contradiction of his gentleness paired with tenacity apparently pushes some big arousal button I didn't know I had.

Being around Oliver is to feel his attention on you, keen and focused. He seems to excel at existing in the present moment. Impressive, as when not otherwise occupied, my mind constantly heads back in time, reliving past traumas, past hurts, regrets, loss, pain, even when my current situation is fine, or more than fine.

Here I am doing it again, unable to stop fidgeting while he unravels each stitch, as deliberate as unzipping a zipper a tooth at a time. The bodice sags in front when he gets to the top, and I clutch it to my chest to avoid it falling off completely.

"That did it," I say, my voice strangely low-pitched. "No need to work on the other seam."

Oliver hands me the seam ripper carefully. "Anything else I can do?"

"No, thanks. The skirt's separate. I should be able to manage."

There's a beat of silence, in which I'm very aware of the ease with which I could drop the bodice in blatant invitation. I'm nearly certain that Oliver would accept it. He'd kiss me and crowd me against the wall and...what? We'd fuck in this bathroom?

I shake my head to clear it of the ludicrous fantasy. Oliver gets the message, backs his way to the door. "I'll wait outside. Call if you need me."

"Thanks." Once he's gone, I relock the door. I remove the rest of my bridesmaid getup carefully, including undergarments. Quickly I don thankfully plain panties and bra, then jeans I've modified with a piece of elastic in order to fasten, a tank top, and comfy sweater. I slide back into my flats, and leave my hair hanging loose. I curse myself as a fool the entire time for wanting the last person I should be getting physically involved with.

He probably won't even be there when I come out, I rationalize. He'll grasp what a bad bargain he's getting and he'll come to his senses and he'll go back to whatever swanky hotel he's staying at and have his lawyer contact me on Monday.

That's what he *should* do.

And my life would be so much simpler if he did.

But, of course, he's still there, lounging calmly against the wall as if he has nothing better to do with his life than wait for me. His smile when he sees me is quick. Genuine. And even though I feel more like myself now that I'm out of my costume, I'm more out of my depth than ever.

CHAPTER 16
OLIVER

I'm both aroused and guilty for being that way by the time I leave the bathroom. Kate only asked for my help because I was the most convenient option, not because she particularly wanted me.

Right?

When she emerges a couple of minutes later, I've gotten myself under control. We may have already had sex, but we're still more or less strangers, and I'm committed to showing her she can trust me—both with her and our baby. I can tell I've made progress, and I'm not about to fuck it up by trying to get in her pants.

Then I see what she's wearing.

I've only ever seen her wear super feminine clothes—the shiny, painted-on party dress the night we met and the over-the-top bridesmaid dress she's carrying over her arm. But now she's in faded boyfriend jeans and a plain gray tank top with a thin black cardigan over it. At the sight of Kate dressed down I swallow thickly. I imagine her in my favorite Armani button down and nothing else and regret it, because I'm getting hard again. This is so inappropriate.

"What?" she asks, looking down at herself. "Is my fly open?"

"No, sorry. You just look nice." I'm an idiot.

"It feels so good to get out of those clothes."

"I'll bet."

"Thanks for your help."

"Anytime."

What are we supposed to be doing again? Not seducing each other, that's for sure.

"Are you going to drive back home?" she asks.

"Home?"

"Silver Lake, right?"

Oh right, home. Where I live. For some reason I forgot where I live. "No, I have a room at the Biltmore."

She whistles, and I fight the impulse to defend my choice. Yeah, it's pricey. But I was so annoyed at having to go to this wedding in the first place, I decided to treat myself. Usually when I come into town I stay with friends. I decide not to tell Kate that I was hoping I wouldn't be spending the night alone. But maybe she gets that anyway, because her whistle turns into a smirk.

I glance at my watch. It's well after midnight. "So, you need to do anything else or can we get out of here?" The "we" slips off my tongue, but she doesn't question it, so I won't either.

"I should probably find Rosie or Nicole, let them know I'm taking off."

I nod, slip my hands in my pockets. "I'll help you find them."

"Or I could just text them and we could go right now."

"Let me," I hold out my hand and she stares at it, "take your bag."

"Oh." She hesitates. "Thanks." She gives me the handle of her rolling case, redistributes the weight of her other bag and her dress. "You know, dinner feels like ages ago and I don't think I actually ate much. I'm starving. What about you?"

"I could eat." It doesn't matter if I'm hungry or not. I'll do anything to stay with her.

"It's so late. What's even open around here?"

I forgot she's not local. It's strange that both times we've met a hundred miles from where we live. But if there's one thing I do know about Santa Barbara, it's the restaurant scene. There's only one place we can get food at this hour.

"I know where we can get a fantastic burger. You game?"

She puts her hand over her stomach and I track the movement, coveting both her and the bump I imagine on her abdomen. "I'd kill for a burger right now. I'm in."

* * *

I worry Kate might bolt in the time it takes to get my Mercedes from the valet and load her bags into it. But it seems she's made a decision, or she's just really jonesing for a burger, because she tells me she'll come back for her car later. She climbs into the passenger seat. Fog's rolled in, chilling the midnight air, so I flick the seat warmers on when I see her shrinking into the leather seat.

"This is quite a car." She looks around as if looking for something nice to say about it.

"Thanks."

"Aren't you worried about fuel economy?"

"I drive a motorcycle most of the time. My bike gets great gas mileage. This is for special occasions."

She laughs. I don't.

"You're joking, right?"

"No, I only drive this when I can't take my Ducati. It gets about forty-five miles to the gallon."

She sucks in a breath. "No, I mean you really drive a motorcycle?"

"Yes." Is that bad? Have I just disqualified myself as father material?

There's a long silence. I'm following GPS through the dark twisty roads of Santa Barbara, heading toward the beach. The streets are deserted and lit only by my headlights. It feels like we're the only two people on earth.

"Please tell me you at least wear a helmet."

"Of course I wear a helmet. It's an Arai. It's SNELL-certified."

"That means nothing to me."

"It's safe. I'm a good driver."

"Yeah, but you can drive as safe as anything and you can't control what other people are going to do. Someone could run a red light and you could—"

"Everything in life comes with risks." I've had this conversation with every woman in my life since I learned to ride in my early twenties. I did it right, took classes, started on a beginner's bike. I don't take unnecessary chances and I love being able to zip through traffic and not sit in the parking lot of cars that is Los Angeles at rush hour.

"Yeah, but—you know what, never mind."

"Have you ever ridden a motorcycle?"

"I did for a part once."

"What did you think?"

"I was in a very controlled setting. There was a stunt coordinator and a ton of safety checks and I didn't actually drive the thing—I was on it for all of an eighth of a mile probably."

"But wasn't it crazy fun?"

"It wasn't not fun," she says begrudgingly, as if I'm pulling the words out of her with a hot poker.

"I'll take it." I merge onto a main road. Not long now before we get where we're going.

"So does housesitting mean Nicole and Ricky have some adorable but neurotic rescue dog you have to take care of?"

"No pets. I think they offered it to me so I'd have some-where to crash."

"Then you're welcome to stay with me, if you want." I pull the Mercedes to a stop in front of the valet stand at the Spanish Colonial-style hotel.

Kate looks at me skeptically. "The burger you promised me happens to be at your hotel?"

"Room service. Only thing open all night in this town. I've done the market research."

"I believe you. And I'm just hungry enough to overlook this blatant play to get me to spend the night with you." She sounds more amused than mad, so I shoot her as innocent a grin as I can muster and hand the car over to the valet. I let the bellhop take the bags out of the back, her small case, my overnight bag. What are we paying for if not the service? At the desk, I discreetly arrange for a room with two beds instead of the king I reserved, and place the burger order right there so it won't be ages before Kate gets her meal.

Less than ten minutes later we're ensconced in the sitting area of a spotless, spacious suite on the second floor of the main building. Kate relaxes the moment she sees the separate beds, which makes me both more relaxed and a bit regretful. I think about changing into my sleep clothes, but that would be weird, right? In the end, I take off my socks and shoes, and pour us some water from a glass bottle in the fridge.

"You're rich, aren't you?" Kate's tone is wry, like she should have seen this coming.

"Financially stable, I think I said."

"Yeah, but you're drinking bottled water from the minibar at the Biltmore without batting an eye. I think that means you're in the one percent."

"I'm not in the one percent, I promise. But we're celebrating, and I'm not going to cheap out on the mother of my child by making her drink tap water."

"I like tap water." But she drinks from the glass I give her anyway.

"The tap water around here tastes like chemicals. New York's is so much better."

"That's where you're from? New York?"

"Upper East Side."

She snorts. "One percent."

"Where did you grow up?"

"Sherman Oaks."

"That's not exactly Skid Row."

"No, but I didn't go to Harvard Westlake, if you know what I mean. My mom's an accountant for a production company and my dad was a camera operator for years until he hurt himself on a job and couldn't work anymore. We're solid Valley stock."

"You don't have an accent."

"Neither do you, unless it's that pseudo-European one you slip into sometimes."

"Hey, I come by my Euro-trashiness honestly." I waggle my eyebrows, give her my best brooding European look, thumb and forefinger stroking my bearded chin. "Bonjour, bébé." My lips purse in an exaggerated pout and Kate laughs, her eyes lighting up like stars. The arrival of room service rescues me from doing something dumb, like kissing her.

The burgers are big and hot and overpriced, and I'd pay a hundred times as much just to watch Kate's face melt into ecstasy as she bites into hers.

"Oh my God, this is incredible," she groans with her mouth full of food.

I nod, not tasting mine. Kate's the sexiest woman I've ever shared a meal with in a fancy hotel room. Is there something wrong with me that I think she's adorable even when she's talking with her mouth full?

We eat for a while in comfortable silence.

I open a comically tiny jar of ketchup, dip a fry right in.

"So, what sort of food will you have at your restaurant?"

"Mercy SB is a contemporary take on French-inspired California cuisine with some North African elements." The elevator pitch slides off my tongue. Kate wrinkles her forehead.

"That's what we tell the investors, but it's not as stuffy as it sounds. We're bringing a lot of the favorites from Mercy and Mercy West Hollywood with us, but all the North African stuff is new. Jamila, the chef, has Moroccan heritage, like me, so we've got some rad tagines on the menu." My mouth waters thinking about one of the simple one-pot dishes that combine the classic flavors of lamb, dates, and cinnamon. "We're also going to serve updated classics, boeuf bourguignon, cassoulet, all totally local, grass-fed California beef, sustainably raised geese, local garlic, you get the idea."

"Sounds amazing. Do your parents cook?" Kate's finished her burger and moved on to the fries.

"My parents are excellent orderers. They have every decent restaurant in Manhattan on speed dial. They should have stock in Grubhub. Though my dad does make incredible scrambled eggs. My mother never learned to cook, but she has impeccable taste. She's given me some notes on the menu already."

"And what about you—you cook?"

"Enough to know I should leave it to the experts, at least when it comes to my restaurants."

"I like to cook," she says. "But I don't do it enough. I used to more, when I wasn't cooking for one. Ben was a vegetarian, though, and I never quite mastered the art of tofu."

"You won't be cooking for one anymore." It just comes out. I guess my filter is shot. "I mean…"

"I know what you mean. And you're right." She puts down the French fry in her hand, wipes her fingers on the hotel napkin.

"Your parents, do they know about the baby?"

"Uh, no, I haven't told them yet."

"How do you think they'll react?"

Her face clouds over. "I think they'll be surprised. Probably they'll be happy. Less so when they work out that just because I'm having a baby I'm not necessarily in a relationship. My mom's basically been pushing for me to start dating again since the funeral was over. I don't think she wants me to end up a spinster."

"Do people end up spinsters anymore?"

"Oh sure. It's not pejorative. Or at least that's what Ophelia used to say before she fell in love. How's your family going to react?"

"Honestly, they'll probably be thrilled. Babies are very big in my family, and my brother's twins are two now, so they're aging out."

"I'm going to have to meet your family, aren't I? If, you know, that's something you—"

"Of course you're going to meet my family," I break in. "They're going to love you."

"Well, that's a given," she says, then laughs. Her laugh is full-throated, even when it's self-deprecating. I'm captivated by the line of her neck, that graceful curve, and by her perpetually rosy cheeks.

I must be staring at her because she says, "What? Ketchup on my face?"

"No. Sorry. It's just—" I can't tell her she's the most beautiful woman I've ever seen. "Hey, you must be exhausted. We should probably go to sleep."

"This has definitely been a long day." She looks at the room service tray, which between the two of us we've made a big dent in. "Thanks for feeding me. I needed that."

Hearing that soothes the part of me that needs to give her everything, anything. I puff with an unreasonable feeling of pride. I can order room service. Go me.

"I'll just—" She stands up, goes over to her suitcase, looks at it uncertainly.

"Do you want me to drive you to Ricky's?" She has to know she has the option.

"Do you want me to leave?" There's no judgment in her tone.

I cast about for the right words to convey how very much I don't want her to leave, and finally settle on, "No."

"Then I'll just take a quick shower." She disappears into the bathroom, along with her entire rolling suitcase. The lock clicks behind her.

I busy myself with tidying our dishes and putting them in the hallway. I specifically do not think about her stripping down, standing under the hot spray of water, or consider what it would be like to join her, soaping her mile-long legs, washing her profusion of silky hair. I don't think about that at all as I hastily take off my wedding guest attire and change into soft gray pajama bottoms and a white T-shirt. I usually skip the shirt, but I'm acutely aware of my desire not to make her uncomfortable.

I have no idea which bed she wants, so I choose the one nearer to the window, leaving her the one closer to the bathroom. I plug in my phone and pull a book and reading glasses from the outside pocket of my bag.

I'm sitting up reading a Catherine the Great biography when Kate emerges from the bathroom in a pair of lavender-colored shorts and a white tank top, her damp hair pulled back and plaited into a braid that falls over one shoulder. She looks about sixteen, blooming and lovely. I look down at my book but I don't see the words.

She climbs into the other bed and turns on her side toward me. "You wear glasses?"

"Just to read."

"Me too."

"Astigmatism," I say.

"Nearsighted."

"We'll have to keep on top of the baby's eye exams. My astigmatism was caught late and my parents thought I had a learning disability. Turns out I just couldn't see properly."

"Oliver?"

"Yeah?"

"Why are you being so calm about all this? It's unreal."

"I don't know. It just feels like the thing to do."

She doesn't respond. I've got to go brush my teeth. I've never been able to sleep without clean teeth. I set my book and glasses down on the night table, swing my feet to the floor.

"Oliver?" she says again.

"Yeah?"

"Come here?" She reaches out her hand, and I push off my bed and end up kneeling in the space next to hers. Her outstretched hand finds my arm and holds on. She leans in and kisses me.

Kate tastes like toothpaste and smells like soap, clean and fresh. Kissing her now is nothing like kissing her the first time, when she tasted like tequila and lime juice and the promise of sex. Sex has nothing to do with this kiss. Right now, it's about closeness, and comfort, and an aha feeling of fitting together.

We trade those soft, comfortable kisses for a while, and it feels so good to be allowed this close to her. Then her tongue darts out, touches the corner of my mouth, and I let out an involuntary groan. I hadn't realized how close to the edge of something else, something hotter and deeper, we were. I curse myself for not keeping that part of my desire for her under tighter wraps, because at the sound I make Kate freezes. I don't move either. She started this, she has to set the pace. It's the best kind of surprise when she starts moving again, her tongue sweeping into my mouth, soft and seductive and so, so perfect.

But the tang of her mint toothpaste reminds me that I still

taste like onions and ketchup and I won't continue to inflict that on her. I pull back, reluctantly. "Hey, I'm going to brush my teeth, okay?"

She lets go of my arm like she's only now aware she's holding me. Her eyes are round, the blue of the irises hypnotic, but I manage to get to my feet and turn around to hide the evidence of how hot I found those few minutes of gentle kissing.

I sort of stumble into the bathroom, fumbling for the light switch, not bothering to lock the door. I get my breathing under control, grab my toothbrush. What are we doing? What does she want? Does she even know? Do I?

I attack my teeth with the brush like they've personally offended me. My thoughts are going a million miles an hour, the gears in my head turning uselessly. None of this really matters. What matters is Kate and how well we fit and have right from the start when I first saw her across a crowded room and all that jazz. I rinse my mouth, toothbrush clattering to the countertop.

I throw open the door, determined to pick up where we left off, and leave the overthinking for another day, but Kate's bed is empty. Her suitcase is gone, and so is she.

CHAPTER 17

KATE

I'm an idiot. A sleep-deprived, hormone-addled, clueless idiot. And things were going so well.

Now I'm running away at two o'clock in the morning, no transportation, phone with 5 percent battery, wandering the halls of the most expensive hotel in Santa Barbara in my jammies. This is definitely a low point, and I've had some doozies.

One minute, everything felt like it was going to turn out okay, the next minute I'm epically screwing up. What was I supposed to do when I discovered Oliver reading in bed, wearing glasses? Glasses are just playing dirty. How many versions of Oliver are there, anyway? And why does every single one make me want to climb him like a tree?

At first I thought he was enjoying the kissing, until he escaped with the unconvincing excuse of brushing his teeth. How could I have misread the situation so badly? He'd gotten a room with two beds and barely touched me all night. I'd confused his gentlemanly caretaking with personal interest, and mortified us both in the process.

Leaving might not have been the most mature thing to do.

It's not even the first time I've walked away from him tonight. But this was definitely my least well-thought-out exit.

I get into the elevator, hesitate before punching a button. Maybe I should go back and face my humiliation head-on. I could at the very least change back into my jeans. God, what is it about Oliver that twists me up like this? Before I can decide, the elevator doors ping back open.

Oliver's on the other side. He looks dreadful. His hair's messy and he's wearing his dress shoes without socks, holding his phone and nothing else.

"Jesus Christ, Kate. Are you trying to give me a heart attack?"

"No—I, I'm sorry." Suddenly, I'm crying. He wraps his arms around me and I sag into him. I want to apologize, to tell him that I'm the rock, I'm not supposed to fall apart and run away and cry. But I can't say a word.

He holds me and walks us back to the room, managing to bring me and my bag, too. As soon as we're safely back inside, he turns me to face him. "Please, please, don't disappear on me like that."

"Okay." I sniff, and a tear escapes my eye. He darts forward, kisses it before it rolls all the way down my face. He kisses below my other eye, and then the corner of my mouth, and then we're kissing in earnest, hot and desperate.

His tongue touches mine, and I pull back, surprised. "You brushed your teeth."

"Of course I did. What did you think I was doing in there?"

"Trying to get away from me?"

He presses a kiss to the corner of my mouth. "Never."

"Oh."

"Yeah. Oh."

I kiss him again, to show him I believe him, to prove to myself that everything I feel when we're kissing is real. It feels real, like we're meant to be doing it, but that's such a foreign concept I almost have to turn my brain off in order to follow through. The first time, I had alcohol to smooth away the doubts. Tonight, I have no such assistance. I'm stone-cold sober, yet this feels more right than ever.

We don't stop kissing on our way to the bed. I collapse onto it gratefully. Oliver's lips are soft; they soothe and inflame at the same time. The soft press of them warms my skin, chased by the searing heat of his tongue. He pulls my bottom lip between his teeth and sucks, plumping it up. No two kisses are the same, and I constantly crave another, wanting to hit the button and find out what else he has in store for me, to find out which kiss I like best. So far I like them all the best.

Every kiss is new territory, and every single one deepens the ache between my legs. I'm sticky and wet, drenching the thin cotton of my sleep shorts, my arousal unmistakable. Some prudish part of me doesn't want him to think I'm this turned on by kissing, but the part of me that wants him to take the edge off wins out. I grab his hand and press it to the wet fabric and the mound underneath. He takes the hint, sliding his fingers underneath my shorts, mapping out my wet folds and ridges expertly until he's finally rubbing the spot where I yearn for the most friction.

He kneads my clit ruthlessly, never letting up the assault on my mouth, until I'm writhing underneath him. I wrench my mouth from his long enough to say his name, a broken whimper I'd be embarrassed about if I weren't coming so hard I see fireworks behind my squeezed-shut eyes.

"That's right, come on." He keeps up the pressure, letting me ride out the orgasm on the flat of his hand, his other hand wrapped around the nape of my neck, supporting me as I curl toward him like a leaf toward sunlight.

The first thing I see when I open my eyes are his kiss-wrecked lips, red and wet, and the wave of lust I experience is so strong it shocks me into action. I pull him down on top of me, his erection clearly outlined through the soft material of his sleep pants. I grab his ass as he ruts against the ruined fabric between my legs. He moves his arms, trapping me between them as he rolls deliberately over my still-sensitive clit with the long hard line of his cock. I spread my legs to give him better access.

He squeezes his eyes shut. "Fuck, Kate."

"Yes. Please." I've just come, but I want more. This is how it was the first time. We were together for only a handful of hours, but we managed to pack a lot in. That was new for me. I'd chalked it up to my severe drought, but maybe this is simply how we are together. One frantic coupling doesn't come anywhere close to sating our need.

He seems on board with the suggestion, but he doesn't move, just keeps up the maddening roll of his hips. I have to tip the scales. I cross my arms and yank at the hem of my tank, pulling it over my head as quickly as I can. My action exposes the width of my belly, not noticeably more curved to anyone but myself, and then my breasts, which have always been half blessing, half curse, the generous proportions of them never failing to draw attention. Men love my breasts. Oliver is no exception, but he doesn't reach out to touch, not right away. Instead, he stills his rolling motion, tips back so he's kneeling between my legs. He matches me, whipping his own shirt up and over his head. I'm enthralled by his strong torso, with the fine black hair dusting his chest, concentrated more heavily below his belly button, leading into the waistband of his pants.

I take advantage of the pause to wriggle out of my shorts, hoping that if I'm totally naked, he'll follow suit and we'll finally get to the main event.

"You are..."

I'm on tenterhooks waiting for him to finish the sentence. Instead of words, I get his palm on my jaw, the sweep of his thumb over my lips. I shiver as he trails his fingers down the side of my neck, across my collarbone, swirls them around my nipple, causing it to shrink and tighten in anticipation. He visits the other, until I'm sporting a pebble-hard matched set. My gaze locks onto his face, a mask of concentration as his fingers leave me for the waistband of his pants.

Finally.

"Let me get a condom."

"Oliver, I think that ship has sailed." It's not like we can't still use one, but I need him to be inside me, like, yesterday.

He rolls his eyes, climbs off of me. I prop myself up on my elbows, annoyance rippling through me. I'm naked and wet and starving for orgasm number two and he's going to get a condom that we don't even really need. I can't get pregnant twice, and I'm sure that despite our slip-up in April, he's normally careful. So careful that he's getting a condom to fuck a girl he's already knocked up.

I watch him go into the bathroom and try to banish the sliver of insecurity that led me to flee the last time he left me to go in there. He's back in less than ten seconds with a couple of foil squares in his hand.

So he's sensible. That's something I didn't expect—for him to be the sensible one. The Oliver I've built up in my head is a roguish playboy who wouldn't say no to a beautiful girl who wants him to fuck her with nothing in the way.

"There are lots of doctor's appointments in our future, right?" he says. "Let's get clean bills of health first."

I reel at the implication that we're at the start of something long-term here, both because of the baby and because this isn't some pity fuck or stress release or proving something to ourselves. I'm not ready to examine what this is instead. I just nod.

He shucks off his pants, *finally*, and I watch, blatantly curious, as he rolls the condom on. He's thick and uncut and I wish I hadn't been so demanding about him fucking me because I want to know what it feels like to have him in my mouth, but there's time for that later. Apparently.

He climbs back on the bed. The sharp tang of the condom cuts through the haze of sex smells, and I wrinkle my nose. I hate that smell. It reminds me of college and sleeping with guys I was half-heartedly interested in. Until Ben.

Then Oliver's mouth is on me, licking broad, messy stripes from my pussy to my clit and I shudder, but he doesn't give me a chance to recover before he kisses his way across my belly, ghosting a kiss over my belly button, nuzzles at my breasts lightly, each one in turn, then returns to my mouth. I taste myself on him, a little sour, and it's incredibly hot. What's hotter is the way the blunt head of his cock is nudging at my entrance. He pauses, holding back until I meet his gaze. "Kate?"

I'm impatient and don't especially want to respond verbally, but I know he won't do it until I give him what he wants.

"Please. I need it, Oliver." I sound whiny but I'm past caring.

He smiles a little. "You need it?"

I try to slide closer, to impale myself on him, but he won't let me. The tip of his cock rests on the cusp of entering my body, teasing me, torturing me. "Yes, I fucking need it."

"What do you need, Kate?"

So many answers to that question. I say the one that comes immediately to mind.

"You."

It must be the right answer because he kisses me and thrusts. My cry of pleasure goes straight into his open mouth.

It's not long before I feel the orgasm build to a point where I can simply surrender and let my body spiral past the tight, needy feeling and into something lighter, freer. I'm flooded with endorphins, my mind blessedly blank, my body just a vessel for liquid pleasure.

He stops kissing me long enough to pant my name over and over. "Kate, Kate, I have to—"

His hips stutter and I urge him on, my hands digging into his flank, until he stops moving, stops speaking, and all that's between us is the ragged noise of our breathing, his hot breath on my neck, my heart starting a slow descent from the frenzied heights of my orgasm.

The condom at least makes cleaning up a bit easier, though there's no way I want to put my damp shorts back on. Instead, I pull on my top and grab a pair of clean underwear from my bag. Oliver dumps the condom and I hear water running in the bathroom. He comes back into the bedroom with just his sleep pants on, no shirt.

Wordlessly, I scoot over. He gets into bed beside me. I click off the light. I have no idea what time it is, but it must be close to dawn, because when the light goes off, the edges of the curtains are outlined with gray light. I haven't stayed up this late since college.

Oliver shifts, bunching up a pillow under his head. Is this okay, us sharing a bed? Before I finish the thought his hand, warm and heavy, comes to rest on my hip. I arch back instinctively, until the curve of my ass meets the concave of his hips. I sigh, and I'm out.

CHAPTER 18

OLIVER

When I wake up alone in the bed, it takes me about ten seconds to become conscious of why that's a bad thing. I jolt upright, looking around for Kate.

"Kate?" There's fear in my voice, but I don't care. She promised not to disappear on me, but she could have changed her mind in the light of day. Obviously sleeping together was a bad move. I should have been stronger, should have told her we needed to wait. I'm not exactly winning points in the self-control department.

I've fucked everything up before it could really begin.

Logic returns when I notice her bag on the other side of the room and register the shower running in the bathroom. I reach for my phone, but it's dead. I didn't bother to plug it back in after grabbing it to follow Kate last night. I do that now, then locate the room's alarm clock. Almost eleven.

I use the room phone to call down to the front desk and request a late checkout and order brunch for two. With the practical out of the way, I'm at a loss as to what to do next. This time yesterday, I was a clueless bachelor complaining about having to attend a wedding. Now I'm a clueless bachelor who's going to be a dad and who's way too into a woman who has a pathological need to do things on her own.

Last night, I had just been trying to make sure she didn't cut me out and dismiss me as an accidental sperm donor. But that was before we slept together, before I had the taste of her on my tongue, before I remembered how unbelievably satisfying it feels to make her come.

If things were different, I wouldn't hesitate before inviting myself into the shower with her, getting us both soapy and slick and getting off before breakfast. Our knees would be weak from orgasms and hunger and we'd sit around, naked under our hotel robes while we ate in bed, trading sips of coffee and hash brown-flavored kisses.

But that seductive fantasy seems like a future-Oliver-and-Kate thing to do. We've gone from zero to sixty faster than the 2.8 seconds it takes my Ducati to get there, and if all we keep doing is trading angsty looks and fucking our brains out, we're not going to have much of a foundation for the next couple of decades of co-parenting. I have to stay focused if I'm going to convince her that I'm not just playing around.

So, no shower sex.

While I wait for my turn in the bathroom, I set out my clothes for the day and check my email. I'd been planning to return to Silver Lake on the early side, but there's something I want to do in Santa Barbara first.

Kate and room service appear at the same time. I'm gratified by the look of excitement on Kate's face when she comprehends I'm feeding her again. She looks lovely this morning. Her hair has been freed from the braid and hangs in loose waves over her shoulders. She's wearing the same jeans but a different top and there's nothing on her face but a little lip gloss.

"Help yourself." I point to the food. "I'm going to shower. Please stay until I'm finished?" I hold her gaze until she nods. I can't say I'm not a little nervous about leaving her alone, but I have to trust her. Still, I shower in record time and don't bother trimming my beard like I normally do. Instead, I just comb it, rub a little beard oil in—no point in looking completely unkempt. I dress in jeans and a white button down, as casual as I get. It's Sunday, after all.

Kate's still there, having made a decent dent in her meal. I follow suit, not even minding the by-now cold eggs, because Kate's raving about the coffee and offers me the pot.

"You know what, let me," she says, reaching for a cup. "How do you take it?"

"Black is fine," I say, enjoying the graceful way she tips the pot over, a steady stream of life-giving caffeine filling up the china cup.

"I drink mine black, too."

"We have a lot in common."

"How so?" She tips her head to the side in question. "Besides the fact we're going to be parents to the same human?"

I'm impressed with the casual way that little bombshell rolls off her tongue and keep my tone light in response. "We're both reading-glasses-wearing, black-coffee-drinking millennials who like to dance."

"Aren't you a little old for that generational designation?"

"Ouch. I'm technically still a millennial. I like avocado toast. I have charcoal-activated toothpaste."

"Gross."

"I know, it's so disgusting. It looks like I'm brushing with a lump of coal."

"Then why do you do it?"

"Because I'm a millennial! Fad toothpastes are in the fine print on the membership card."

That gets her to laugh, and I'm way prouder of that outcome than I should be. I try to be as casual as I can when I ask, "I don't know what plans you have today, but I was wondering if you would come with me someplace?"

"That's not sinisterly vague or anything," Kate says with a smile. "But no, I don't have plans. I was so focused on getting through the wedding that I figured if I survived, I deserved a day off. I have to work tomorrow, though."

"Podcasting?"

She narrows her eyes at me. "Are you sure you're a millennial? Have you even heard a podcast before?"

"Of course I have!" I struggle to remember the name of any podcast I might have inadvertently listened to.

"Uh-huh. I'll make a playlist for you, shows I think you'll like."

"Your work?"

"Some of it. You know, there are a lot of food and drink podcasts. I produce one about local beer—*Brew O'Clock*."

"Oh! I've actually heard about that one. My friend Mike told me it was great exposure for his brewery."

"Exactly. Wait, you're friends with Mike O'Dowd? He was a really good guest. Very natural and funny."

Am I imagining it, or are Kate's cheeks pinking up a little? It takes me a second to recognize the stab of discomfort I feel around my midsection as jealousy. I don't usually hang around girls long enough to care who they think is "natural" or "funny." But with Kate, I care about everything.

"I've got to say, if your friends are as cool as Mike, then that bodes well."

"Does it?" I remind myself that showing her we have stuff in common is my whole goal here. I should be happy that she approves of my friends.

"Anyway, you'd probably like that one. There's also *Copper and Heat*—that won a James Beard award—and *Gravy*, about food in the South. Oh! And Nicole's friend River's partner is starting a show about the Santa Barbara County restaurant scene—I bet I could get you on as a guest."

"River who owns Denim? I met them last night at the wedding."

"Oh, nice."

"It seems like you know a lot of people in Santa Barbara considering you're an Angeleno."

"What can I say? Nicole sort of draws everyone into her orbit. I feel like I've been up here every other weekend since she sprung this whole bridesmaid thing on me."

"You didn't want to be a bridesmaid?"

"None of us did, not really. But we love Nicole, and we knew resistance was futile."

That description seems accurate, given what little I know of the woman myself. "Was it worth it?"

"She's my best friend. She and Ricky were both there for me when Ben died, so there was no way I couldn't do it."

She doesn't look particularly sensitive talking about Ben this morning, but I choose my words carefully. "They probably didn't think you owed them anything."

"I know. But I wanted to be there for them, too."

Kate's loyal, and willing to put her own emotional well-being on the line for her friends. I'm impressed with her strength, but I wish she'd had someone to act as a buffer between her and Nicole's hurricane-like personality. If I'd been in the picture, I could have made sure that she was setting up some boundaries, getting the self-care she needed to get through the ordeal, which no doubt raised a bunch of feelings in her.

I can only wonder how Nicole's going to deal with Kate leapfrogging ahead of her in the baby department. Better to keep things out of the deep end right now and change the subject. "Speaking of Santa Barbara and restaurants..."

"Oh?" She smiles, acknowledging my awkward segue.

"That's where I want to go today."

"To a Santa Barbara restaurant? We just ate."

"To my Santa Barbara restaurant. I want to show you Mercy SB."

"Oh." Her smile softens. "Okay."

We tidy away the dishes, then brush our teeth side by side in the bathroom like an old married couple, one of whom has bought into the trend of brushing his teeth with something that looks like compressed fireplace ashes.

Despite constantly being distracted by how incredibly gorgeous she is, being with Kate isn't like being with anyone else. I avoid relationships because the women I hook up with aren't exactly people I want to hang out with and have long conversations with and talk to about my work. They're pretty and available and fun. Kate's not entertaining, not really. She's work. And since I'm not afraid of hard work, it seems like that's right up my street.

I just have no idea if she feels the same way.

CHAPTER 19

KATE

Everyone get home okay last night? No major hangovers?

I'm good. So glad that's done.

O

Not *too* hung over. Jamie's still asleep. I think he had too many Irish coffees.

Nicole texted me, btw. They're at the airport. She's still riding high.

She's going to crash.

Lani! What the hell?

Not literally. 🙂 I mean she must be exhausted. I hope she sleeps the whole way to Paris.

Sorry. I'm tired, too. Maybe I'll go back to bed.

ROSIE

Anyone heard from Kate?

Kate?

LANI

Bueller?

She's fine. She's probably sleeping. Like the
rest of us should be.

O

Yeah, don't worry, Rosie. Enjoy your day off—
no work and NO WEDDING STUFF!!!

ROSIE

You're right. Thanks.

Also, Kate—text me!!!

* * *

On a sunny Sunday in June, the Funk Zone is packed
with pedestrians of all ages crowding the sidewalks
outside the bars, restaurants, bakeries, and little shops. The
Funk Zone was once an industrial district, but eventually its
proximity to the beach and its walkability from State Street
doomed the area to gentrification. Still, it's charming, and the
beer offerings are excellent. Too bad I can't have any.

There's never enough parking even when it's not peak
hours, but Oliver pulls into an almost invisible alley so narrow
I'm afraid the paint's going to scrape off the side of his overpriced gas-guzzler. But it seems he's done this before, because
the alley opens up behind the building. The alley view of
Mercy SB is unassuming, another squat, metal-sided, proto-
industrial rectangle, with a Dumpster and broken-down card-
board boxes and rubber kitchen mats drying on the chain-link

fence that separates the property from the screen-printing shop next door.

"When do you open again?"

"Soft opening in a little over three weeks, grand opening a week after that."

"Wow, that's soon."

"Tell me about it. Nat's adding three things to my to-do list for every one thing I get done."

Oliver uses keys to open the back door, then punches some numbers into a keypad. It's dark and cool inside.

"No one's working today?"

"My manager's been hiring staff all week. I told her to take the weekend off."

He flicks on some lights and walks me to the kitchen, a massive, gleaming space that's surprisingly bare.

"How many covers will you be aiming for?"

Oliver lifts an eyebrow.

"What? I know a smidgen about this stuff." One of my early gigs was a restaurant review podcast that petered out after a couple of months, but I picked up some of the lingo.

"We can do 250 a night."

"Just dinner?"

"To start it'll be dinner service only, but we'll add Tuesday through Sunday lunch once we get things squared away."

"Is that how your other places are?"

"That's how they started. I can't believe you've never been to Mercy. I need to target our marketing to the millennial podcast producer segment." He shows me his dimple.

I can't help but laugh. For being a serious restaurateur and fairly intense guy, Oliver can be funny. Oh hell.

My stomach rolls, and not with morning sickness. It's occurring to me how many stupid boxes Oliver checks for me. Not to start with the superficial, but since that's what got us into this mess, yeah, he's hot. He's an off-the-charts kisser. We're definitely sexually compatible. He's hardworking and creative and willing to acknowledge when he's wrong. He's also protective and gentlemanly in an old-fashioned sort of way that sometimes makes him seem like he's from a far-off land. Maybe that's his parents' influence, since they weren't born in America. New York isn't exactly a foreign country, but to someone whose high school prom date wore skateboard shoes and a clip-on tie, the Big Apple is exotic.

"You okay?"

I shake myself out of my pointless mental monologue. It doesn't matter if we're compatible and he's hot. It doesn't even matter that we slept together less than twelve hours ago, and even though he hasn't touched me or kissed me yet today, I would do it again in a heartbeat. We're not getting together like that. I'm supposed to be simplifying things, figuring out how to do them on my own. Won't having total control over my baby's future be simpler? Oliver just brings complications.

"Sure, I'm fine."

If I tell Oliver I'm one step from losing it, he's going to want to do something about it. He's going to want to fix it. I'm scared that if I let him help me, I'll stop being able to help myself. And when he leaves, I'll be flattened. I don't know if I can build myself back up again after that. Coming back from Ben's death was the hardest thing I've ever had to do. I don't think I could do it again.

He's been opening and closing drawers, inspecting their contents while we talk, but suddenly he stops and walks over to me. I lean against one of those sterile, smooth tables, cool under my touch. He gets close, boxing my legs in between his, resting his hands lightly on my hips. It should make me feel trapped, but instead I lean into his touch.

"I'm beginning to understand that 'fine' is Kate-speak for freaking out." He doesn't demand, but he also doesn't leave any room for me to evade.

"You figured it out. My secret code." I shrug carelessly. "Good for you."

"What are you thinking about?"

"I'm thinking I want to see the rest of this joint. What's the dining room like?"

He frowns at me. "Are you feeling okay, you know, physically?"

"I'm—" I start to say fine, then relent. "No, I feel great, truly. I slept amazingly well. I'm not even hungry. Right now."

He smiles at the last two tacked-on words. "Okay, let me know. I like feeding you."

"I noticed."

We look at each other for a beat. He's so close I can discern the different shades of brown of his eyes, lighter around the edges. I can practically make out each individual eyelash, thick as they are. Kill me now. Thick eyelashes—so not playing fair. Ben's eyelashes had been kind of sparse, but I'd loved him anyway. See, I'm not shallow.

I wait for Oliver to say something, and when he doesn't, I wait for him to kiss me. And when he doesn't do that, either, I finally open my mouth.

"You're right. I was having a tiny freak-out. 'Fine' used to be a reach goal. For about a year I was so depressed, 'fine' was like this shining beacon in the distance that I could only aspire to. Then therapy started actually making me feel better instead of being a place I cried for an hour every week. 'Fine' was attainable again. Then all this wedding stuff started, and I won't lie— I backslid a little. I was pretty low the night of the bachelorette. The night we met?" I put the question into my voice, even though I know he remembers. I wait for him to nod.

"Being with you was something I needed, I guess. Even though, yeah, I freaked out and left you hanging. It was still... nice. Then I found out about the baby, which was... unexpected."

Unexpected is such a dramatic understatement that I laugh a little.

"Then you showed up and you've been really patient with me, and not what I imagined at all, and I'm just afraid that these feelings, feelings that are so much more than 'fine,' are fake or they're going to disappear or something. They can't be sustainable. I don't really know what to do with feeling this... good. So, yeah. I'm not fine. I'm better than fine. And that freaks me the fuck out, Oliver."

He hasn't moved, except to rub small circles on my sides where his hands are still anchored. If I've frightened him with my honesty, well, better I know now that he can't handle the real me when I'm not running away or deflecting or kissing him to get him to stop asking me questions.

"So, you're saying—" he pauses, licks his lips "—you're happy? And that you like me?" He says that last part with such boyish hopefulness that I have to seal my mouth shut in order not to laugh.

"Yes, Oliver, against my better judgment, I like you."

He smiles at that, as if he really wasn't sure of my answer. "Can I kiss you?"

"I don't think too clearly when you do."

"That means I'm doing it right."

"But doesn't all this—" I gesture between us, as if that communicates something "—make things more complicated?"

"Does the fact that we're attracted to each other make the fact that we're having a baby together complicated?"

"Yes, that's exactly what I mean. Thank you."

"I don't know. Maybe it makes things easier." He lifts the hem of my shirt slightly so his hands can rest on my skin. His thumbs stroke my hipbones and I shiver.

"That sounds like the rationalization of someone who wants to get in my pants."

"I'm definitely guilty of wanting that. But that doesn't mean my reasoning is flawed."

I tip my head back when he starts nuzzling under my ear, either to get away or to allow him better access, I'm not sure which.

"I don't think you know what you're saying," I say, though it's getting hard to string words together with the way his tongue is flicking at my earlobe.

"Sorry, I'll stop," he says, pulling away from me.

"Well, you don't have to go as far as all that." I kiss him on the mouth and we stand in his restaurant kitchen, making out for what feels like an hour, until my lips are chapped and hot to the touch, my cheeks scraped despite the softness of his beard. My panties have long since been soaked through by the time we lift our mouths off each other, breathing heavily. Oliver's erection has been nestled, hot and solid, against my hip for the past however long, but he's made no move to get either of us off. He seems content to drug me with kisses, and I'm powerless to argue.

"Checking out of the hotel was dumb."

He laughs into my neck. "We'll survive."

I sigh skeptically. "If you say so."

He really and truly lets go of me then. "Come on, I'll show you the dining room and then we'll figure out the rest."

"What rest?"

"All of it."

As vague and grandiose as that is, when I fit my hand into his and follow him into the dining room where he's going to be serving 250 people a night, I almost believe him.

CHAPTER 20
OLIVER

The day is going by way too fast. We finish Kate's Mercy SB tour, and yes, I'm aware I am shamelessly showing off —I want her to like it. Her insightful questions and quiet praise make me happier than they probably should.

Even though our breakfast was more like lunch, we grab burritos from a food truck that's pulled into an empty lot between the restaurant and the beach. A beer would be the appropriate accompaniment, but in solidarity with Kate I order horchata instead. I persuade her to walk down to the water, so we cross the train tracks, eating our lunch and dodging cars, until we're cruising along the sandy sidewalk that parallels the Pacific. Sunbathers, kids, kite flyers, and skateboarders are out getting their share of vitamin D for the day. Kate's so fair I worry about her burning, but she pulls a baseball cap and sunglasses out of her purse. I can't believe how glamorous she looks, even in baggy jeans. I bump her hip with mine.

"You look like Audrey Hepburn."

"What? No, I'm too tall."

"Jessica Chastain then."

"Better."

"On second thought, she's come into Mercy a few times, and you're twice as attractive as she is."

Even behind her sunglasses I can tell she's rolling her eyes.

"What? I call it like I see it."

"I have also met Jessica Chastain, and thanks for the compliment. She's one of those actors who's more good-looking in person, isn't she?"

"Did you work with her?" I remind myself to look Kate's credits up on IMDb later.

"I had an audition with her once. Didn't get the part, but she was really encouraging." Kate tells me a bit about what it was like working in TV and movies for the years she was a working actor.

"How'd you get your start?"

"Growing up in L.A., it's sort of in the water. If you have halfway supportive parents and a good acting teacher and you show up on time, you can book gigs. I never had big ambitions, but I always liked that on a set you can pretend you're someone else while people with headsets run around randomly telling you what to do. I think that's why I'm more comfortable behind the scenes now. Podcasting is the ultimate form of expression for introverts.

"So, what was it like growing up in New York?"

I let her get away with changing the subject.

"I can't complain about being a privileged kid growing up in Manhattan."

"So why did you move to L.A.?"

"I left because if I had stayed I would have been living my father's life instead of mine. He expected me to follow him into the family business. I ran away, got a useless History degree, partied for a few years. L.A. itself was mostly about self-preservation. I thought if I could get far enough away, I wouldn't have to face his disappointment." I glance sideways at her but can't read her expression.

"Turns out L.A. suits me. I think I needed the space to make my own way. But it's funny. I'm just now realizing that even though I'm in restaurants instead of wine, I've basically done the same thing as my father after all—built a business."

"It feels good, right?"

"What?"

"Building something out of nothing."

That's what she's done, too, with her podcasting company.

"Hey, we're both entrepreneurs," I say, knocking against her shoulder lightly. "See, something else we have in common."

She doesn't respond to that. "Do you think you'd ever move back to New York? You know, expand your restaurant empire coast to coast? The prodigal son returns?" We dump our empty food wrappers in a trash can, turn around, and head back the way we came.

"Never say never, I suppose. I don't know that I have anything to prove to my father. I'm happy with what I've achieved, and I know he's proud of me, even if he hasn't always known how to show it. It would be nice to be closer to my brother and his family—my nephews are adorable. But I like it here. Plus, my blood's adjusted to the weather. I'm weak now."

"I always wanted to live in Manhattan, even if just for a little while," Kate says, surprising me. "You know the way people take a semester abroad to go to London or Paris or Tokyo? I wanted to go to New York. I almost went, but Ben talked me into going with him to Nicaragua for a semester."

"Weren't you a theater major?"

"I got ahead on my other requirements. It was really interesting." Her voice has something in it, like she's spent a decade convincing herself she made the right decision to go to Central America instead of the city she'd always dreamed about living in.

"You've at least visited New York before, right?"

"I visited Ricky and Nicole there once. But my flight was delayed and I had to get back for a shoot, so I only ended up there for like thirty-six hours. But it was great, jet lag aside. Like a movie set, sort of. Everything's so big, but also small. I loved it."

"We should go," I say, without thinking it through.

"To New York?"

"Yeah."

"You mean, after the baby's born?" She looks uncertain and her voice is shy.

I confess I hadn't been picturing that part, just the part where I'd take her to all my favorite places and walk with her through Central Park. I could introduce her to my friends who still live there, see her face light up when we go to as many Broadway shows as we can cram in.

"Or sooner than that? My parents have tons of room, well, by Manhattan standards anyway, and I haven't been back in forever. Things should slow down after Mercy SB opens, and New York's usually humid in September, but maybe we'd get lucky with the weather…"

She's looking at me strangely, and I mentally replay what I've said for some gaffe.

"What?"

"Nothing." She shrugs. "It sounds…nice."

"Okay." Not exactly the level of enthusiasm I'd been hoping for. I shake off my feeling of unease.

"Hey, can you drive me to Rancho del Sol so I can get my car? Hopefully they haven't had the thing towed."

"Of course."

We barely talk on the way, every step away from the frolicking beachgoers reminding me that this isn't real life, we're not just here for a weekend getaway. I have a ton of work waiting for me at home. I don't have time or room in my life to deal with everything that Kate represents—the responsibility of a child and a more intense relationship than I've ever been part of.

Nat is going to kill me when I tell her that part of my attention is going to be on Kate for at least a little while. Part of the reason I've been so successful is because I'm a driven workaholic with no family and something to prove to my withholding father. Now that things seem to be on the mend with my dad, and I have this instant family, does that mean my work is going to suffer?

I brood all the way back into the foothills. By the time we get to Rancho del Sol, I've worked myself into a slight panic. I have no business planning trips to New York with a woman I barely know, offering her a future when my track record with women is a series of sprints to a clearly defined finish line. With Kate, we were off like a shot, but we've got to settle into something sustainable if we're going to make this work. I've never run a marathon, and I've never been with a woman for longer than a few months. I'm not built for long-distance running. Maybe I'm not built for commitment either.

Kate, as much as she denies being on the lookout for any such thing, is a commitment sort of gal. She's the kind of person who stays with her college boyfriend even after he selfishly drags her to Nicaragua instead of letting her have her dream semester, who stays with him while her acting career is taking off, who's so loyal that she doesn't sleep with anyone for three years after the poor bastard dies.

Or maybe she just loved him that much.

The uncomfortable realization that Kate's stuck with me, a stranger she met at a club, instead of someone she chose to share her life with, to build a family with, burns in my throat like a shot of whiskey that went down the wrong pipe. I've been so busy thinking about how my life is going to change, I haven't thought about it from her perspective.

Suddenly, I'm incredibly grateful she chose to tell me about the baby at all. She could have pretended not to know me, could have ignored me at the wedding, could have successfully avoided me for the rest of her life. I'd never have known. I'd never have gotten the chance to know *her*.

That scares me more than anything else.

Kate's compact is still there, alone in a vast parking lot. I load her bag into the tiny trunk. I have a pang of worry imagining her battling Los Angeles traffic in this fuel-efficient tin can, and belatedly get why she'd been so prickly about my motorcycle.

I slam the trunk closed and we stare at each other, saying nothing. Is this it? Are we saying goodbye? We've spent nearly twenty-four hours straight together.

"So." Kate lingers near the driver's door but doesn't open it. "I'll let you know when the next doctor's appointment is, if you want to come."

"Of course, yeah, I want to be there."

"The office is on Wilshire. Parking sucks, but they have valet if you don't mind paying for it."

"Okay." Why am I letting her end things on this transactional note? Why am I not kissing her? The closeness we've built up over the past day feels like it's evaporating into the cloudless blue sky.

"Kate?"

"Yes?"

"Are you—are you going home now, or—?"

"I'm going to spend the night at Nicole and Ricky's. I don't have a recording session until tomorrow afternoon, so I'll just drive home in the morning."

It's on the tip of my tongue to invite myself over, but I have meetings first thing. It's going to take me long enough to make the drive back with all the other city dwellers tonight.

"Well, okay. Be safe." *Be safe?* How lame can I get?

"You too," she says, kindly not making fun of me.

Fuck this, I'm usually much smoother with women. I try to summon up some of my usual swagger when something else occurs to me.

"You never gave me your number."

"Didn't I?"

"No. I gave you mine, but you didn't give me yours."

"I'll text you right now." She pulls her phone from her bag and types something out. A few seconds later my phone buzzes and I peer down, noting the digits like they're a winning lottery number. She's sent me a picture. I tap on the screen and stare uncomprehendingly at the fuzzy black and white abstract art piece in front of me.

"It's the ultrasound pic. Not much to see, really. See that shadow?" She points to the screen. "That's it."

A rubber band tightens around my heart. The shadow could be anything, but it's my baby. There's some doctor code on the side of the picture, and there's a date there, big as life. The date of conception. The date I walked into a club alone and walked out with the most beautiful girl in Santa Barbara. In California. On the continent.

"Thanks." I could be thanking her for her number, or for the grainy image, or for carrying my child.

But I'm thanking her for giving me a chance.

She's smiling when she climbs behind the wheel. I follow her out of the complex, down the winding road to the freeway, where she gets on the northbound onramp. I head south.

As we drive away from each other, I wish I knew if we're parting as friends, lovers, or something else.

CHAPTER 21

KATE

It takes me all of five minutes to determine that Ricky and Nicole's house is in pristine condition. The plants don't even need water, since Gus re-landscaped their entire property to be drought-tolerant. I do bring in their mail from Saturday, but Nicole is having it held the rest of the time they're in Paris. It takes me another five minutes to check my email and social feeds—I've been tagged in a few wedding pictures, but there's nothing that can't wait until tomorrow.

I pace the sunken living room with its massive wall-mounted flat screen, my mind tossing around possibilities of how to spend the evening. The pregnancy handbook Nicole gave me a week ago is buried at the bottom of my suitcase; I'm not particularly interested in paging through it and learning about everything that could go wrong in the next six months. It's too early for bed. I'm not even that tired. I slept soundly tucked into Oliver's side, and then we did nothing but stroll and eat and talk during the most pleasant Sunday I've spent in recent memory.

My face heats even though there's no one around to see my unease as I relive the painful goodbye of less than an hour ago. We'd been having a nice time, and then he'd said that thing about going to New York, as if we were planning a casual couple's getaway. Does he know how intense that proposal is— the two of us flying cross-country together, staying at his parents', being tourists in the most amazing place on earth?

It had rolled off his tongue so easily. *We should go.* As if it's that simple. If he can be that nonchalant about something that major, maybe we have very different ideas about what's happening here. Sleeping together aside, we're not actually a couple. Are we?

I wonder what Oliver's doing right now while I'm stewing alone in emoville. He's probably stuck in traffic. I'd text him to see, except I have a thing about texting people when I know they're driving. I don't want to tempt them into checking their phones and taking their eyes off the road.

Why didn't I invite him back here, or out for dinner? I'm not hungry, but I am bored, and alone, and I'd go home to Los Feliz right now except that I'm too jittery to sit in a car for two hours.

On a whim, and assuming its members are not currently operating motor vehicles, I thumb through my chats and open the Never a Bride(smaids) thread. With two of our members in serious relationships, the name has gotten a little silly—not that it wasn't silly to start with. We were all so worried that Nicole would use her bride-as-god energy to set us up with potential romantic partners that we banded together to present a unified front. No wedding dates required, thank you very much.

It hasn't really turned out the way we expected. Rosie and Gus have been together since the engagement party and are cohabitating like model millennials. Ophelia and Jamie have been official since around Valentine's Day, but since they were attached at the hip before they ever crossed the friends-with-benefits line, the fact that they're all heart eyes now isn't that radical.

No one, least of all myself, would have predicted that my

plus-one to the wedding would be a fetus, or that the fetus's father would have stuck to me like glue all night. Lani, intimidating, funny, casual-sex-having Lani is truly the last standard bearer of the Never a Bride flag, and I crave her ability to put everything in perspective for me.

KATE

I thought I'd never want to see any of your faces again after the wedding, but it turns out I miss you darn bridesmaids. Anyone free for a drink?

LANI

Are you back on the sauce, Kate?

Sadly, I'm only drinking in my mind. Day(dreaming) drinking?

LANI

As long as I can have a real drink, I'm in.

O

Where shall we imbibe these hypothetical drinks?

I'm at Nicole's and she's got an open bar.

LANI

Be there in 10

O

15

ROSIE

I miss you but I'm at home and I'm too lazy to drive up there.

LANI

It's OK. You don't have to stop having sex just to hang with us.

ROSIE

I'm not having sex!

At the moment

O

We'll miss you, too, Rosie 🥲

> None of you better be driving and texting right now. I'll start making the margaritas and defrosting the cheesecake.

ROSIE

Cheesecake? Be there in 45.

* * *

"We should have scheduled a wedding-debrief-slash-margarita-party anyway," Lani says an hour later. She and Ophelia are drinking real margaritas while Rosie and I have virgin approximations. The cheesecake is still half-frozen, but I predict Ophelia's sweet tooth is going to have her cutting into it within five minutes, thawed or not.

"Nicole's had us so focused, I've forgotten what life without wedding planning is like," Ophelia says.

"Seriously. What am I going to do with all my free time, have a kid or something?"

All three turn toward me with wide eyes.

"What? I'm not allowed to joke about it?"

"No, you are, we just weren't sure..." Ophelia glances at the other two, as if they'd held a secret is-Kate-okay summit behind my back. "How are you feeling about everything?"

"Why? What's with all the furtive glances?"

"You just haven't seemed to want to talk about this much," Lani says. "Three weeks ago you tell us you're pregnant and keeping it, and then nothing. Is it okay to talk about it now?"

"Yes. I want to. If you want to?" I suppose it's implied that in addition to not wanting to get married, none of us necessarily wants kids, either. "I was keeping quiet about it because I didn't want Nicole to feel like I was taking any of the attention away from the wedding."

"God forbid," Lani says with a toss of her head, though I'm fairly sure her sarcasm comes from a place of love.

"Well, I, for one, am curious about the guy you seemed to be spending a lot of time with last night." Ophelia cuts into the cheesecake right on schedule. "He was delicious," she says, licking a creamy crumb off her thumb suggestively.

"Ophelia!" Rosie scolds.

"What, don't tell me you didn't notice that a fine man was chatting her up all night. Who could miss those intense brown eyes that looked like they could see right into your soul?" She shivers elaborately. "So, who is he?"

"His name is Oliver Mercier." I try to replicate his accent and fail miserably. I'll have to download Duolingo and start watching Catherine Deneuve movies. I'm an actress, I should be able to do a French accent.

"How do you know him?" Lani says. "Nicole mentioned he knows Ricky through work."

"Yeah, apparently Ricky is investing in his restaurant. That's what he does. He's a restaurateur. He's about to open one in Santa Barbara, and he has two in L.A."

"So he's a chef?" Ophelia asks hopefully. "I like him more by the second."

"No, not really. I think he can cook, a little. But he's more about finding the right chef for his vision of what he wants the restaurant experience to be like."

"Okay, so why was he on you like a fly on honey?" Lani asks.

"He obviously found Kate irresistible," Ophelia says.

Rosie's got her mouth sealed shut. Normally, I appreciate her discretion and the obsessive level of doctor-patient confidentiality she seems to employ with her friends, whether they're her patients or not, but right now I wish she'd just blurt out what I can tell she's dying to say, instead of making me do it.

"You're sweet, but not exactly."

"Please tell me you gave him your number, at least," Ophelia says. "I know it's complicated since you're all, um, pregnant and everything. But he was really, really cute."

"It is complicated." I lock onto the word. "It's very complicated. Complicated is what it is."

"Kate," Rosie says, exasperated. "Just tell them."

"You tell them," I grumble.

Lani's and Ophelia's heads swivel in unison between the two of us.

"Kate." Rosie would make a great mom. She's aces at the disappointed-parent voice.

"Fine. So. Oliver is the guy I met the night of the bachelorette party. I went home with him—well, not to his house, it belonged to a friend of his, but they were camping or something and, well, anyway. I didn't have his number, but there he was, at the wedding. Because in a state with more people than Canada it totally makes sense that the one-night stand who knocked me up is doing business with my best friend's husband."

"Oliver's that guy?" Ophelia whistles. "Your kid is going to be hella good-looking."

"O!" Rosie smacks her on the arm.

"What? Look at their combined genes!"

"You're probably right." I sigh tiredly. "Oliver's mom was a supermodel."

"Wow." Ophelia takes a huge bite of cheesecake, then talks around it. "This is fate."

I snort. "Fate isn't this fucked up."

"What are you talking about?" Lani asks. "Did you tell him about the baby? Was he surprised? I mean, of course he was surprised, but does he, you know, want to be involved?"

"He took it pretty well. And yeah, he wants to be involved." I still feel bad for trying to get him to take an out before he'd even had time to process. Now that I know him a little better, I'm actually glad he's apparently ready to take this on with me. The fact that I'm not going to have to do this entirely alone—that's terrifying in an entirely different way.

"So what's fucked up?" Lani presses.

I push away my uneaten cheesecake and throw my arm dramatically over my eyes, as if I can avoid their knowing gazes when I tell them what I'm about to tell them. "We slept together."

"No duh," Lani says. "That's how it works. Back me up, Dr. Rosie."

"No, I mean, we slept together again. Last night."

"What?" The shriek is so shrill I can't tell who let it out with my eyes closed. I drop my arm and force my eyes open to face them.

"We went to his hotel. The Biltmore."

Lani coos.

"I know. We had room service. And he'd gotten a room with two beds, which if that was reverse psychology totally worked because I wanted to jump his bones the moment I saw him in reading glasses."

"Ah." Ophelia nods understandingly.

"Anyway, one thing led to another..." No need to mention the parts where I freaked out and tried to run out on him and he went after me and brought me back.

"Gah," Ophelia says, fanning herself. "I'll bet it was hot."

Rosie doesn't chide her this time. She appears as interested as the other two in the details.

"It was pretty hot," I confirm, leaving the rest to their imaginations. "But that's bad!"

"Why?" Three voices in unison, three women looking at me like I'm insane.

"Because it's so confusing. Are we dating? Are we fucking? Does he want to be in a relationship? Do I? How can we be parents and figure out all this other nonsense?"

The silence goes on so long after I stop talking I think I've broken them.

"Kate," Rosie ventures hesitantly, "don't you think you're going to have to talk to Oliver about all that?"

"Oh, balls," I say crossly. Everyone laughs, and some of the tension drains out of my shoulders.

"Still, if he's hot, rich enough for the Biltmore, good in bed, *and* wants to be involved with the baby, I'm not really seeing what the problem is." Lani's voice isn't accusatory, just frank.

Rosie and Ophelia know my story. They know what happened with Ben, if not firsthand, then from Nicole. But Lani's only been in Nicole's orbit for a couple of years, that is, post-Ben. There's no reality for her in which Ben and I were going to live happily ever after.

I envy her so much.

I pull the entire cheesecake toward me and stab it with my fork. "The problem is I kind of like him."

No one responds to that.

"And, if you haven't forgotten, we all bonded over our whole never-getting-married thing. I have a lot of really, really good reasons for not wanting to get into that kind of relationship."

"Hey," Ophelia says defensively, "you don't see a ring on this finger, do you?"

"It's okay, O. You're happy. You're allowed to be happy, with or without Jamie. And so is Rosie, with or without Gus. And Lani here, with or without the flavor of the week."

"And what tasty flavors they are." Lani waggles her exquisitely arched eyebrows.

"The point is, our Never a Bride club might have been half-facetious and I'm super happy for you guys, but it's real for me. I can't do it." I rub my chest absently; my heart feels bruised. "I almost felt lucky when this happened—I'll get to be a mom, have a family of my own, without having to put myself through anything like what happened with Ben ever again."

"You're worried if you love someone again, they'll die?" Ophelia says.

"Basically, yes," I snap, hating my tone because I know she's just trying to understand.

"You're going to be a super overprotective mom, then. From what I gather, moms worry about their kids nonstop, even when they don't have a grief complex." This from Lani.

Jesus, when did it become okay for everyone to start armchair therapizing me? Am I on Dax Shepard's podcast here? Each time they open their mouths it feels like they're grinding their fists into that tender spot on my chest.

"Kate, dear, you know you're allowed to be happy, too? That Ben would want you to be happy?" Rosie's voice is the most gentle, and the most devastating.

I start crying then, because they're saying that because they love me. Ricky said the same thing last night and if my actual therapist were here she'd say it, too. And on some level, some super-healthy, super-well-adjusted level, where being the rock isn't just a pose I adopt to get through the day, but is really me, the Kate who survives and thrives, I believe it.

But on this level, the level I can't seem to transcend, I think being allowed to be happy is a lie because I shouldn't be happy if it's not with Ben. I shouldn't get to move on while he's stopped forever, all of his goals and dreams unrealized. Why should I get to be happy, when he doesn't?

I try to breathe. Lani thrusts a tissue in my face, and Rosie rubs a circle on my back.

Ophelia cuts me another piece of cake. "We're sorry, Kate, we just want you to know it's okay to like Oliver. He sounds nice."

"He's not like Ben at all," I say, surprising myself. "If Ben and I had gotten pregnant, he would have wanted to know all about the developmental stages and the wonky, science-y stuff. Oliver wants to be there for me, but he's more of a sensualist, I think. He likes to feed me. He likes to dance. He dresses like a grownup. Remember how Ben basically only wore Patagonia?" I laugh, remembering the time he wore a windbreaker to my cousin's wedding. "Oliver's an adult.

"It's all so unlikely, isn't it, that a guy I'd pick up at a club would be such an apparently good guy. I don't know him all that well, but I have this feeling about him. He gets me."

The ice in my margarita has long since melted, leaving condensation all over the outside of the glass. I run my index finger through the beads of water, making a trail.

"Have you heard of that happening? Ever? A one-night stand turns out to be someone you could love? The guy who knocks you up turns out to be the one you're supposed to be with, baby or no baby?"

I look up and wipe my finger on my jeans. Rosie, Ophelia, and Lani watch me, their faces variations on a theme. They think I'm going crazy. Maybe I am. Maybe after three years of grief and depression, I'm finally going over the edge.

I laugh nervously and answer my own question. "Yeah. That doesn't happen. That's why I need to keep what Oliver and I have strictly business. And I'm definitely not sleeping with him again." The words sound wrong as I say them. And my chest aches with a definite feeling of something not sitting right. The cheesecake could be giving me indigestion. Or maybe the thought of never being that close to Oliver again makes me sick.

I rub the spot on my sternum that feels like it's on fire.

"Are you okay?" Rosie asks, lifting a hand to my cheek. "You're hot."

"No, I feel..." I cover my mouth. I leap up from the couch

and make it to the guest bathroom in time to throw up my margarita and cheesecake supper into the toilet.

Rosie's there, holding my hair and rubbing my back, and Lani hands me a wet hand towel. Ophelia's got everything edible removed from the living room by the time I hobble back, feeling weak and stupid and incredibly grateful not to be alone right now.

"Was that too much cheesecake or the baby?" Lani asks when we're settled back down.

"Both," I groan. "These hormones are a bitch."

Rosie smiles sympathetically. "It's going to get better," she says.

"It already has gotten better," I protest. "I haven't felt that nauseous in a couple of weeks. Everyone says the second trimester is when you feel the best."

"Everyone's different."

"I'm a mess."

"Want us to go so you can get some sleep?" Ophelia asks.

I don't want to be alone with my thoughts right now. "Um. You know what I really want to do?" They look at me expectantly. "Let's watch a movie and not talk about boys, or babies, okay?"

Lani clicks on the flat screen and starts scrolling through the options. "So not a romantic comedy."

"God, no."

"How about *Die Hard*?" Ophelia suggests. "I love me some evil Alan Rickman."

"That's a Christmas movie," Lani argues.

"*Jurassic Park*?"

"Sold. Dinosaurs eating people sounds just about perfect."

CHAPTER 22

OLIVER

I don't sleep well Sunday night. I didn't hear from Kate, even though I texted her when I got home. It's unsettling to be apart after being joined at the hip for a night and a day.

When I get to my office Monday morning, I remind myself she doesn't owe me anything. She didn't make any promises. And I made no promises in return.

But that doesn't stop me from checking my phone obsessively throughout my meeting with Nat and the PR firm handling Mercy SB's opening. It doesn't stop me from wondering if Kate is still in Santa Barbara, what she's wearing, how she's feeling, if she's back in L.A., if she ate a healthy breakfast, if she wants to talk or maybe have dinner tonight, or—

"Earth to Oliver. Come in, Oliver." Nat's glaring at me as if she's been trying to get my attention for a while. I focus in on her brown eyes, outlined in her trademark tortoiseshell glasses. Nat dresses like a '50s housewife, complete with pocketbook and red lipstick. Today she's wearing a yellow dress with a sky blue cardigan over it, colors that pop against her dark brown skin. I wouldn't take extra notice except the cardigan is the same color as Kate's eyes.

I blink and clear my vision of Kate. "Sorry, what?"

"Mika wants to know if she should try to book you on that new foodie podcast you mentioned?"

"Oh, sure. Great."

"What's it called again?" Nat asks, fingers poised over her laptop keyboard.

"Um." I try to recall what Kate told me about her friend's podcast. "I can't remember, but I'll ask someone who knows." There—a legitimate, non-stalker reason to contact Kate.

Mika and Nat exchange a look, and then Nat pushes up from the table and walks Mika out while I brood at my phone. When she comes back, I block the way to her office. "Got a minute?"

She scowls at me. "I don't know what's gotten into you this morning, but I have a ton of work to do. Go bug someone else."

"Yeah, but I'm your boss. Don't you have to make time for me?"

"Only if it's work-related."

"How do you know it's not work-related?"

"Fine. Come into my office. Let's talk about work."

I follow her like a chastised puppy, flopping down in my usual chair while she takes up residence behind her immaculate desk. For the first year, we worked out of a spare room in the back of the original Mercy, but for two years we've rented office space in Silver Lake, equidistant from our respective homes and the two Mercy locations.

It's true that I own 60 percent of the company, she owns 10 percent, and the rest is held by investors like Ricky, but when push comes to shove, everyone knows Nat really has the final say in business matters. When it comes to the menu, staffing, and location, I usually get my way, but only after I've proven that my way is what's best for the bottom line. Nat makes me work harder than I've ever worked in my life, and I'll forever be grateful for that.

She also knows me better than anyone else in L.A. and I'll go crazy if I can't tell her what's gotten me so twisted up on this fine Monday morning.

"Aren't you going to ask me about the wedding?"

"I knew you didn't want to talk about work." She opens her laptop, preparing to ignore me.

"You sent me there for work, remember? I did my job. I congratulated Ricky, met his enchanting bride. She loved me." I decide not to mention the part where Ricky threatened to destroy the company if I hurt Kate. He was being metaphorical. Probably. "I made some good contacts. There's that photographer I mentioned to Mika that I want to cover the opening, and some of the local business owners want to collaborate on promos and events in the fall."

"Good job, boss," she says, only mildly mocking.

"The podcast idea, that came from someone else I met at the wedding."

"Who?"

"One of the bridesmaids. Her name's Kate Treanor. She's a podcast producer. A successful one. She does *Brew O'Clock* and *Diary of a Container Gardener*."

"Really? *Brew O'Clock* is hilarious."

"You listen to podcasts, too?"

"Of course. What do you think I do on that horrible commute every morning?"

"What are you talking about? It takes you fifteen minutes to get here."

"Fifteen minutes I'll never get back," she says with mock solemnity.

Save me from sarcastic women.

"So can she get you on this foodie podcast? Can you call her?" Before I answer her, she narrows her eyes at me. "Oh good lord, you slept with her, didn't you?"

There is no way I can answer that question truthfully and stay on message. My lack of response speaks for itself.

"It turns out I met her before, a couple of months ago, but I didn't get her number, and she didn't get mine, so we lost touch." I don't know why I'm bothering to sugarcoat this. Nat knows my track record, and she's not fooled by me dancing around the issue, if the height of her eyebrows right now is any indication. "Nat, I have to tell you something and you can't tell anyone else yet but I need your perspective."

She grimaces. "I don't want to hear your kinky sex secrets, Oliver."

"No, it's nothing like that. Well—"

"For real. If we had an HR person, I'd be marching into their office right now."

"Nat, come on, I'm being serious. I need your help. You know me better than anyone else. You can tell me if I'm being crazy. Please?"

She really looks at me then. "Okay. I won't sue you. But if this has to do with freaky heterosexual sex, I'm expecting an extra large bonus this year."

"Kate's pregnant. I'm the father. She told me at the wedding and then we talked practically all night and we slept together again and I think I'm falling in love with her."

I didn't know Nat could make that high-pitched of a sound. But the little squeal she emits after I blurt out my confession is nearing dog-level decibels.

"And before you ask, no, I haven't had a paternity test done yet, but I saw the ultrasound and the dates match up. Plus, I trust her."

"It's not that. We can deal with that. I'm sorry, but did you say you were falling in love with her?"

"I said I think I'm falling in love with her. I *think*. That's not the same thing."

"Still, Oliver, I can't believe it!" The grin on her face is confusing. Is she upset with me, or happy for me?

"Believe what?"

"You've never mentioned love in relation to any female except your mother in the entire time I've known you. I wasn't sure you knew what it was."

"Well, that's the problem. I've spent my entire life avoiding falling in love. Now I think it's happening without my consent and I don't know what to do. I mean, I can't stop thinking about her. What do I do?"

"Oh, wow, this is heavy." She takes off her glasses, rubs her eyes, puts them back on. It's a move I've seen her do in meetings when she's trying to bridge a budget gap or deal with a difficult vendor. "Do you think she might feel the same way?"

"I don't know. How can I tell?"

"It's not like figuring out if a kitten is a boy or a girl. You have to ask her, dummy."

I wince. "But what if she doesn't?"

"Then you deal with it and move on. But you said she slept with you after telling you she's pregnant with your baby—congratulations about that, by the way, I always thought you'd be a good dad—so she probably likes you at least well enough to have sex with you."

I try to untangle all the threads of that sentence and give up. "The sex is not the problem." That part, at least, we'd been on the same page for. And it had been a pretty amazing page.

She visibly cringes. "I don't want to hear it."

"But thanks, about the dad thing. Do you really think so?"

"I have to be honest and say that you've always been such a slut that I didn't think it was on your goals list, so it's not something I gave a lot of thought to. I figured you'd be the cool uncle to Marc's kids, but being the cool aunt is kind of my thing, so I'm glad you're going to have your own kid to spoil."

"What? I'm not going to spoil my own kid."

Nat peers over the top of her glasses. "Want to bet?"

"Whatever." That's a battle for another day. "I'm just glad you don't think it's totally wild. The dad thing, I mean."

"Well, it's out of left field, but that doesn't mean it's bad." She looks at her phone, and I have a feeling I'm about to be dismissed, but all she says is, "You're going to want that paternity test, though. And to talk to your lawyer. I'll make you an appointment for later in the week."

That's the Nat I know and— "Hey, about what you said before? That I only say I love my mom?" I wait till she's looking at me to finish. "I love you, you know."

Her smile is quick and surprised and free of any of her usual prickly attitude and, huh, maybe I haven't done a good job of showing her how much she means to me.

"I love you, too, babe."

I beam at her. "So, if me about to be a dad isn't crazy, then falling in love isn't crazy, either?"

She hesitates and my heart squeezes at the implication. She thinks falling for Kate so soon is nuts. It probably is. I suppose I wanted her to tell me to go for it, or something equally idiotic.

"I don't know, Oliver. It would be...out of character for you," she says carefully.

My heart tightens another notch. "So, what? I'm making up these feelings?"

"You said you didn't know if what you were feeling was love. Just give it time. There's no rush to figure this out right now."

I shake my head. That's not how I do things. I get ideas and make them happen. I don't wait around. I act. I see something —or someone—I want and I go for it. Usually we only want each other for a short amount of time. But with Kate, I wanted her that night in the club. I wanted her at the wedding, before I knew about the baby. After I knew, it was like I didn't just want her, I *needed* her. I still do. I especially need to know she's safe and healthy and that she has everything she wants. So maybe what I'm feeling isn't love, it's some hyper-protective thing where I don't want anything bad to happen to the mother of my child.

That explanation makes intellectual sense, but it still leaves me feeling bleak.

"You're right. No rush. No need to label things. I'll just, uh, let it play out."

Nat frowns. "You okay?"

"What? Yeah. No. I'm fine."

"Okay. We have to get through the next few weeks until the opening and then maybe you should take some time off. It sounds like you're going to be dealing with a lot."

"Time off, that's not a bad idea. I was just talking with—" I stop myself from saying her name. "I mean, I was thinking of going to New York to visit the family."

"You should definitely do that," Nat says assertively. "Let's pencil it in for August. No, better make it Labor Day. Tickets will be more expensive, but it'll be better for your work schedule."

"Okay." Conversations with Nat, as always, end with practical matters, names and places and dates and to-do lists.

When I get back to my own office, I force myself to focus on the pile of things I have to do today.

I do not text Kate.

CHAPTER 23

KATE

Life returns almost disturbingly to normal the week after the wedding. There are no emotional emails from Nicole, only a brief text that she and Ricky are having a fabulous time in Paris. Work keeps my mind off everything else, with everything else being the baby, Oliver, and what the hell I'm going to do about him.

I never responded to his text letting me know he arrived in L.A. the other night, and he hasn't texted me since. I pick up my phone about six times an hour, but when it comes down to it, I can't figure out what to say.

I finally break my silence after I schedule my next doctor's appointment, two whole weeks away. My fingers are clumsy and I have to erase every word twice because I can't seem to spell anything right on the first try.

> Hi Oliver, it's Kate. My next doctor's appointment is set for Wednesday the 8th at 10 am. I hope that's convenient for you. I'll send you the address. See you then!

I cringe after I hit send over that last, pathetic exclamation point and my bizarrely formal tone, then go back to my exciting afternoon activity of washing dishes. He texts back so quickly I jump when my phone buzzes on the kitchen counter.

OLIVER

That is convenient. Thanks for arranging it.
How are you feeling?

I'm doing well, thanks

Please let me know if you need anything. I'll be
in SB this weekend, but I can make other
arrangements.

I'm sure that won't be necessary. But
thank you.

Of course

I bite my lip and reread our excruciatingly polite and stilted exchange. It's like we're business partners instead of people who've fucked—spectacularly—twice. This is what I'd expected all along. These annoying negotiations are why I was hoping to avoid having a partner in all of this. My profound disappointment at him keeping me at arm's length isn't appropriate.

I get through the week somehow, working on setting the recording schedule through the rest of the summer. The entire time I'm looking at the calendar, Oliver's casual suggestion we visit New York together echoes around my head. Should I take the idea seriously and block off some time around Labor Day? If we wait any longer, I'll be in my third trimester and won't be able to fly. In the end, I don't check with him, but leave a week free. I deserve a break, even if I end up spending it alone at home, or, more likely, with Nicole dragging me to prenatal yoga or something.

I'm actually looking forward to her getting back. Even though we live 100 miles apart, Nicole always makes time for me. With the wedding dispatched, I'm at sea. I don't have anyone local that I can talk about this with, having let most of my L.A. friends disperse in the wake of Ben's death.

For a moment Oliver made me feel like I wasn't going through it alone anymore. He'd been so reassuring. Even if neither of us knew what the hell we were doing, he made me think we'd figure it out together. If only I could leave it at that, take what he was offering—support, a practical partnership— and forget his eyes, his smile, the way he moves when he dances. If only I could forget the look in his eyes when he's about to kiss me.

Of course, he offered me more than just support. He offered me his bed, his body. I know that could continue to be part of the package, for a while at least. But despite the decisions I made that led us here in the first place, I know in my bones that the whole package isn't in the cards.

Saturday I make the short trek to the Valley to the house where I grew up, a one-story ranch house off Van Nuys, with an avocado tree in the backyard and an orange tree in the front. My sister lives five streets away with her police officer husband and two-year-old daughter. We get together for takeout every few weeks. I arrive before Kelly and Chris and little Riley, help Mom unpack the dozen sushi rolls, seaweed salad, and miso soup, plus chicken teriyaki for Chris, onto the kitchen island while Dad watches Wimbledon in the living room.

Mom asks about the wedding.

"Nicole looked stunning in the picture you sent. What on earth are you going to do with all your free time, now that it's over?" She's joking, but not. My parents have always been a little intimidated by Nicole and her wealthy Santa Barbara society family.

"I wanted to wait until Kelly got here, but I do have some news."

Mom looks at me sharply. I meet her gaze, feel the weight of blue eyes identical to my own staring at me from a face lined with age but still attractive. She could have been in show business if she'd wanted to, but she's never liked being on the receiving end of attention. She likes working with numbers, making things add up right, keeping things nice and neat. Ben's death wasn't neat, and it hurt her that she wasn't able to fix it as easily as a broken spreadsheet formula. It's only in the last eighteen months or so, when I've been able to function more or less normally, that we've reached the equilibrium we used to have.

"News? About work?"

"No. But your idea about me hiring an assistant—I think I'm ready now." I'll need someone I can trust when the baby comes. "Will you let me know if you come across anyone good?"

She smiles, at her most comfortable when she can help me with something practical. "Sure. Raj's son just graduated and I know he's looking."

"Raj, our neighbor's son? Little Darsh?"

She laughs. "Little Darsh is twenty-two and about six feet tall."

"God, that makes me feel so old. I remember when he was born!"

Kelly bursts into the kitchen. "Remember when who was born?"

"Darsh," Mom says. "Grab some soy sauce from the fridge, Kelly?"

If I resemble our mom, she's a miniature version of our dad, round-faced, straight blonde hair, sturdy build. Before she can get to the fridge, I pull her into a hug, squeezing hard, surprising both of us.

We've always been the kind of sisters who were supportive and nice to each other, but we've never been super close, probably because with our four-year age difference, we were never in the same stage at the same time. Things got even weirder when right around the same time that Ben died, Kelly and Chris decided to get married and had Riley a year later. I felt like her life was working out while mine had stalled, and it was hard for me to let that go.

Mom takes two plates of food into the dining room, and I grab the rest. Kelly gets the soy sauce and pours a glass of milk for Riley.

"What's up? Why were you talking about Darsh? Going on a date?"

"Ew, no. He's nine years younger than me!"

"So? He's cute. I saw him mowing his parents' lawn the other day. Very yummy."

"Oh my God." I giggle, then consider. "Really?"

She shrugs. "See for yourself."

"Well, Mom thinks he might make a good assistant for me."

"Oh, no, then you won't be able to hit on him!" She frowns in mock consternation.

We're laughing as we bring the plates into the dining room, and I feel lighter than I have around my family in a long time. It wasn't that long ago that I wouldn't have been able to joke with my sister about a cute guy. The memory of Ben was too fresh, and the very idea of someone else, even casually, would have set me off into a crying jag.

"Jack, Chris, get in here," Mom calls.

"Federer's playing." Dad grumbles, but he shuffles in obediently.

"It's only the quarter finals," Mom says. "Here's your teriyaki, Chris."

Chris is stocky and fair, not that different from Dad, though he's thirty years younger. Since his injury, my dad's aged a lot, but he's great with Riley, who climbs up on his lap to steal food from his plate. She must be hungry, because she plows into the rice with her chubby toddler fingers, making an instant mess. I plant a kiss on her baby-soft blonde hair as I take up a seat next to her and Dad at the table.

"Oh, I forgot, Chris, would you like a beer? I have Sapporo," Mom offers.

Chris nods. "Sure, I'll get it, thanks. Want one, babe?"

My sister nods, leans over the table to wipe some rice off Riley's chin.

"I know Jack'll have one. What about you, Kate?"

"No, thanks." I smile, suddenly excited about the reason I can't drink. "Actually, I want to tell you guys something."

Chris pauses on his way to the kitchen. Mom looks up. Riley doesn't stop shoving rice into her mouth. Dad's got one eye on the sliver of the television screen he can see from the dining room, and one eye on his California roll. Kelly trades her chopsticks for a fork; she's never been able to master them.

"I'm pregnant."

CHAPTER 24

KATE

Mom and Dad don't react right away, but Kelly shrieks. "What? Oh my God. What?"

"I'm having a baby."

"How? What? When are you due?" Kelly's still the only one talking, but Chris sits back down, beer apparently forgotten.

"Around the New Year. And as for how…" I don't exactly want to explain to my parents that I had unprotected sex with a one-night stand, but hey, we're all adults here. Except for Riley. I glance over at my niece, but she's happily engaged in chasing rice around her plate.

"You got a sperm donor," Mom says matter-of-factly.

"I hope you picked someone smart," Dad says. "That's one of the choices, right?"

"Did you pick someone hot? Do you get to see their picture?" Kelly's never really gotten less boy crazy, even after marrying the love of her life.

"I did not get a sperm donor," I manage to spit out through my consternation.

"Sperm donor!" Riley says with glee.

"Jesus," Chris says. "I'm getting those beers." He disappears into the kitchen. I hear the fridge opening and bottles clinking, but I doubt he'll rush to come back.

"Sorry to disappoint you all, but it happened the old-fashioned way."

"So you're in a relationship?" Mom asks with surprised pleasure.

"Er, no." My stomach plummets at the flash of disappointment on her face.

"Here's what happened." I stop, not sure how to go on. All eyes are on me. Even my dad is watching me expectantly. I guess a pregnancy trumps Federer. Telling them I got drunk and picked up a random guy at a nightclub is too humiliating to bear. "I have this friend. Oliver."

"Ooh, classy name." Kelly's hanging on every syllable.

"And we had a night together and no, we didn't plan this, but we're both happy about it." That's true enough, isn't it? "We're just friends but we're going to raise the baby together." *I think.*

My mom's forehead has about a million creases in it as she processes, while my dad asks if Oliver is employed.

"He has his own business, like me," I say. "He owns restaurants."

"Restaurants are money pits," Dad says automatically.

I suppress a smile at locating the source of my own preconceived idea on the subject. "His are successful, apparently." I looked up Mercy online this week and read some reviews. Apparently Oliver manages to "combine impeccable service and inventive food without sacrificing a hospitable atmosphere."

"Is he cute?" Kelly practically begs. "Do you have a picture?"

"What does it matter?"

"You're right, any baby you have will be adorable," she says. "I was just wondering."

"He's very attractive," I grit out. I don't have a picture, but there's one on the Mercy website. I pull it up on my phone, because Kelly won't let it go until I do. "See?"

She gasps. "Oh my God. Look, Mom!" She thrusts the phone at Mom who blinks at the photo calmly. "He's dreamy."

"His mom's Moroccan. She's a really famous model," I say. "His dad's French. They live in New York."

This makes Mom frown.

"But he lives in Silver Lake."

She relaxes a bit.

I take a long-awaited bite of my sushi, nearly choking on it when Kelly yelps again, startling me. "Stop!"

"What?"

"You aren't supposed to eat sushi when you're pregnant."

I swallow my bite. "Why not? It's my favorite."

"Raw fish? Salmonella and listeria and all that potential bacteria?"

"Seriously?" Shit. I thought the hard part was getting through three months of feeling like I had mono, followed by childbirth. Now I have to spend the next six months not drinking *and* not eating sushi?

"Well, just to be on the safe side," she says. "Here, have some of Chris's teriyaki."

"Hey!" Chris pokes his head through the kitchen door to protest his wife's co-opting of his meal.

"I'm fine, really. Not necessary. I'll see what's in the fridge." I stand up and escape to the kitchen as Chris comes back to the table. My face feels hot and my stomach is unsettled from the conversation. I can all but feel bacteria colonizing my gut, poisoning me and my baby.

I've never had to think about food this much before. Before, the only things I had to worry about were if my eggs were free-range and my meat was grass-fed. But now food seems to be the enemy, with its newfound ability to make me sick and potentially damage my baby.

I squeeze my eyes shut. It's too much to handle on top of not knowing how to explain Oliver to my family. The friends who accidentally slept together and got pregnant story seems to have been accepted, but it's not really the truth. I'd like to think that Oliver and I are friends, but how can that be? I've never been friends with someone I wanted to kiss so desperately before.

I splash some cold water from the sink on my face and turn around when I hear someone enter the kitchen. It's Mom, who goes to the fridge.

"I have some leftover lasagna. Want me to heat it up for you?"

"No, I want sushi." I sound like a petulant teenager, which is understandable when standing in the kitchen of the house I grew up in, my mother offering me food. Ugh. "Sorry. Lasagna sounds good."

She moves around her kitchen with practiced economy.

"Why did you jump to the conclusion that I got a sperm donor?"

She doesn't look at me, finds a fork in the silverware drawer and closes it with her hip. "Ever since Ben died, I've been hoping you would eventually be able to move on enough to not miss out on your own life. You had me worried, baby. But you've always done things your own way." She cuts me a generous piece of lasagna and sticks it in the microwave.

"You wanted to try acting, but you also wanted to go to college. You got engaged instead of dating people in the industry who'd be good for your career. And you gave it all up when Ben died. Then you built something new. I'm really proud of you for finding a new path for yourself.

"I knew if you really wanted a baby, you'd find a way to do it. And you did."

I never considered that. On some level, could I have *wanted* to get pregnant during my first and only one-night stand? I shake my head. No. I'd been too drunk to be thinking that strategically.

But she's not wrong. I did want a baby. Now I'm having one. I could have gone the donor route or the adoption route. Maybe I would have some day.

"So you're not upset I'm doing this on my own?"

"You're going to be a great mom, and Dad and I will help you if you want us to. We love being grandparents, and you're going be awesome at this. Okay? Never doubt that."

I smile. "Thanks." I didn't know how much I needed to hear that she thinks I'm going to be a good mom, but I feel lighter than I have in days.

"And if the dad—Oliver—is just a friend, but you think he's going to be a good dad, then that's peachy. But I'm going to say this, because I'm your mom and I'm allowed to give you advice once in a blue moon." She looks at me, sadness and love in her eyes. I'm suddenly nervous about what she might say.

"Please know that you don't have to be alone forever. A kid doesn't take the place of a partner. Don't let this be another reason you stay alone. You have so much love inside you, Kate. You've got enough to love this baby, and to love someone else, too. You even have enough to keep loving Ben forever."

My heart aches in that old, familiar way. I rub a spot over my breastbone to soothe it.

"You can do this alone. I have no doubt. But don't use it as an excuse. Don't stop looking for someone else to love. You've got plenty of love to go around."

I draw in a tremulous breath when she's done. I want to argue with her, to tell her she sounds like Nicole, spreading the gospel that we're all better off when we've paired up with our soulmates. It's easy for them. It's all they've ever known. Nicole has Ricky. Mom has Dad. Kelly has Chris.

And I had Ben.

Not everyone gets to keep what they have, apparently. But I can have something else.

As if engaging in mother-daughter telepathy, Mom puts up a hand. "Don't shut down the possibility. Someday. You don't have to look for it today. You just have to promise me you won't fight it if it comes."

"I can't," I whisper. "Don't make me promise that."

Her eyes fill with tears. "Baby. I wish I could explain—well, you'll find out soon enough—how much it hurts when you can't take the pain away from someone you love more than life."

"Well, fuck." I sniffle. I've been focusing on the short term—getting through morning sickness, telling Oliver, figuring out how to keep doing my job after the baby comes. I know I'll be tired and overwhelmed, but it'll be worth it because the cute, tiny baby will be there to make it an adventure. I've been thinking about the happiness, about the joy. I haven't thought about the pain. I've had enough of that for an entire lifetime. But now it seems I'm taking on more.

But I'm strong. I'm the rock. I can handle it. I'll have to. And despite Mom's best intentions, I'm going to do it alone.

CHAPTER 25
OLIVER

Somehow I get through the days until Kate's doctor's appointment. I wake up early, hit the gym every other day on my way to the office, and eat breakfast hunched over my laptop the other mornings. Work keeps me grounded, wears me out, pushes the constant, nagging worry about Kate and the baby to the back of my mind.

Nat doesn't bring up the baby, but she does add an appointment with my lawyer to my calendar. When I meet with her and explain the situation, she immediately advises me to draw up a new will, which I agree to do. But when she suggests outlining a custody agreement, I balk. It's too close to Kate's initial suggestion of hashing everything out through lawyers.

I hope I've convinced Kate by now that she can depend on me for more than a child support check, but it's confusing to have the logical part of me see the need for boundaries while my heart wants to keep all my options open.

I'm up at the new restaurant five times. On the drive between L.A. and Santa Barbara I listen to a sampling of Kate's company's podcasts. Each one is funny, sharp, with outstanding production values. She's good at what she does. I'm not one iota surprised.

Even though it's not her voice in my ear, it sort of feels like she's keeping me company. I imagine what it would be like, her sitting in the passenger seat and telling me behind-the-scenes stories of the podcast we're listening to, laughing over gaffes and outtakes.

Instead, it's just me and my phone and endless cars snaking north, brown hills on my right, a shimmering ocean on my left.

"This is bullshit." I click the button that pauses the audio, hover my finger over the text icon, before I pull back and refocus on the road in front of me. Kate wouldn't want me texting and driving. I force myself to wait until I get to Mercy SB, but the minute I arrive there's a crisis with the meat vendor that I have to sort out and the moment is lost.

* * *

I arrive thirty minutes early to the doctor's appointment, spending the extra time pacing nervously in the lobby of the building like the super suave man I am. But Kate shows up early, too. She looks sensational in a blue skirt and white top, the picture of summer on this July morning. She's hope and fun and laughter and family and sex and dreams and need and yes.

"Kate." In my eloquence, that's all I can say.

She inclines her head in greeting. "Oliver."

We don't say anything else, but she takes my arm when I offer it as if we're a courting couple about to take a turn about the park. She hits the floor number in the elevator and we ride up in silence. I don't care if we don't talk. The uncertainty and worry I've been shadowed with for the past two weeks have been chased away by the light that is Kate's presence. I'm happy just to be with her.

When we get to the office, Kate checks in, murmuring to the receptionist. I loiter awkwardly, glancing around the waiting room. A middle-aged woman flips through a magazine. A youngish couple peers into the bulky plastic carrier on the floor between them. A pterodactyl-like cry rises up and I work out that there's a baby in there. I edge closer. A loaf-of-bread-sized person swaddled in a yellow blanket opens and closes its mouth, its pale-tea-colored face puckered in seeming consternation at being subjected to the world at large. The mom rocks the carrier with her toe while the dad takes a picture of the baby with his phone.

"How old?" I ask.

"Two weeks," the mom says. She looks tired, but there's a smile in her voice.

"Almost brand-new," I say inanely.

The dad snaps another picture. "He's already gained back to more than his birth weight."

I nod, as if that means something to me. "Congratulations."

"Thanks," they murmur in unison, still staring at their child.

Does having a kid make you dopey and lovesick? I straighten up and look at Kate, who's watching me with a little smile on her face. I sigh. Probably. There was no hope that I wasn't going to be dopey over our kid the moment Kate told me it existed.

There's no point in pretending I'm not dopey over her, too.

I follow Kate in when her name is called by a brisk nurse in unfortunate olive-green scrubs, feel profoundly ill at ease as she's ordered to step on a scale, the numbers read out loud and clear. Next, she's ushered into a bathroom to pee into a cup while I stand in the hallway, shifting from foot to foot, self-conscious and out of place. I have no right to be in this domain of women.

Eventually, we're shown into a room. The nurse slaps a disposable gown on the examining table and disappears. Kate, graceful through it all, clears her throat delicately. I turn my back while she takes off her skirt and trades it for the noisy paper gown. She's nonchalant, as if this is something she does all the time. I can't even remember the last time I went to a doctor.

"And you have to go every month?" I was shocked when Kate had shared that fact.

"Every week when you get closer to the due date."

"Jesus." I thought I could handle this, but I'm not impressing myself with my togetherness right now.

A long moment passes in complete silence. Why are we being so quiet? Why can't I think of anything to say? I look at Kate helplessly. I'm capable of a lot of things, but I'm pretty damn far outside my comfort zone right now. What made me believe I could casually waltz in and be a superb partner to her? I'm so unprepared. I should have done research, should have loaded up my phone with books about pregnancy and read them in every spare minute. I should have, hell, not assumed I knew anything about this process whatsoever.

I open my mouth to apologize, to swear I'll do better, but Kate speaks first.

"When I was little and we were waiting for the doctor, my mom played this game with us. I Spy?" She tilts her head in question and I shake mine.

"I spy with my little eye," she says slowly, as she scans the little room, "something blue."

I blink. The entire room looks blue to me.

"Now you guess what I spied."

"Seriously?"

"Just do it, Oliver."

"The walls."

She rolls her eyes, disappointed at my obvious guess. "No."

I try harder, unsuccessfully guessing the soap dispenser and the blood pressure cuff before I figure out she's not going to pick something that easy. I take a second look around the room.

The brightest blue in the place is the color of her eyes, but since she can't see those, it's probably not the answer.

"Give up?" she asks.

I wrench myself away from staring at her pretty face and glance at the floor. I'm wearing blue suede sneakers. "My shoes?"

"Got it!" She seems way too proud of me for finally winning this dumb game. "Your turn."

I pretend to look around, but I already know what I'm going to choose. "I spy with my little eye something pink."

"Pink?" She frowns and looks around. "Is it that uterus?" She points to the poster on the wall above the sink that features a cross section of female anatomy.

"Nope."

"Tissue box?"

I shake my head.

"Parenting magazine?"

"No."

"Hmmm. This is a tough one. You're tricky."

"I learned from the best."

"Well, that's true." She glances down at herself, to see if I've taken a page from her playbook, but there's nothing overtly pink.

"I give up."

I walk the two feet from where I've been resting against the counter to the table where she's sitting with her perfect posture. "Your lips," I whisper.

Her fingers fly to her mouth, makeup-free and the color of young raspberries. "No fair. I can't see those."

I shrug and tap the corner of my eye. "I spied them with my little eye, remember?"

She gives me a grudging smile. I like this meaningless banter, and even if I should be thinking of other things, while we're on the topic of her mouth, it would be a shame not to kiss her, just to see if she tastes as sweet as I remember.

I lean slightly forward and her eyes widen. "Can I—"

The knock at the door makes me jump back. It flies open to reveal the doctor, a middle-aged woman with frosted blonde hair and a scarily firm handshake who introduces herself as Dr. Sorensen. I melt to the back of the room, partially relieved that we'd been interrupted. I can only imagine that if Kate thinks I can't keep it in my pants at a doctor's office, what type of a father she assumes I'll be.

"Okay, Kate, you're here for your fourteen-week checkup, and we're going to draw some blood so we can establish paternity, correct?"

She nods, glancing sideways at me, her expression unreadable.

"Well, it's straightforward. We'll get samples from both of you and we'll have the results in about a week."

"Really? That's so fast," Kate says.

"Miracle of modern science," Dr. Sorensen says. "We can even determine the baby's sex, if you want to know now."

Kate and I look at each other. "Yeah, I mean, I guess I want to know. Do you, Oliver?"

"Sure, why not?" This is so surreal. In a week I'll know if we're having a boy or a girl. I don't need the paternity test to tell me I'm the father.

"Okay, you two. Hold tight."

I slip my hand over Kate's and squeeze. I'm holding tight and I don't want to let go.

CHAPTER 26

KATE

Blood drawn, swab taken, clothes back on, we're dismissed with our next appointment on the books and a promise to be notified with the test results as soon as they come in.

Then we're back in the lobby, about to pay a hefty ransom for the return of our vehicles. Oliver seems quiet. I imagine the experience we've just had is reinforcing the enormity of what we're taking on.

Any second I'm expecting him to bail, to say, *You know what, I'm good. Let's sign a paper and call the whole thing off.* Part of me wishes he would. It would make my feelings for him a lot less relevant.

He merely glances at his watch and asks, "Can I interest you in some lunch?"

I check my phone. I could probably squeeze in a short meal, but I have a recording scheduled. "I have to get back to work. Another time?"

"I'll hold you to that," he says with an easy smile.

Dammit. I walked right into that one. "I'm sure you will."

Lunch would have been nice, but too disorienting. I would have wanted to just be with Oliver, the cute guy I'm getting to know, instead of processing the fact that I'm growing a person inside me. The doctor's visit unsettled me, not just because everything is so real and I'm going to be a mom in the blink of an eye, but also because I'm fairly sure that Oliver was about to kiss me back there. He was certainly flirting, which seems to be his go-to mode.

I know we've slept together, but I'm still not sure that makes me different from any girl Oliver would be enclosed in a small space with.

The valets bring the cars around, Oliver's luxury monstrosity and my well-used compact. Another study in contrasts. I'm not saying he needs to be a Ben-level tree-hugger, but is it too much to ask that he drive a hybrid at least?

He gives me one of those European cheek kisses goodbye, the kind that make most people look like posers but he manages to deliver with authenticity. Goddammit.

My gut churns with baby hormones and mixed feelings all the way back to work.

* * *

OLIVER

Lunch today?

Working, sorry.

Friday?

Friday works.

Village Bakery. Noon.

Make it 12:30.

Until then.

* * *

It both irks me and impresses me that Oliver arranges lunch so easily. Twelve thirty isn't necessarily better for me than noon, but I have to put my foot down about something. I've been to the venerable Atwater Village café a million times, but all my go-to parking spots are filled. I have to circle the block twice before I find a slot on a residential street that leaves me with an inch to spare before verging into illegal. I speed walk to the bakery, sweating in the ninety-degree heat. I hate being late, and I detest the feeling of going into a meeting with Oliver even slightly not at my best.

I round the corner and spot a shiny black and red motorcycle parked right in front of the café. It wasn't there the first time I'd lapped the block. Oliver is standing there taking off his helmet. Of course he'd arrive on time, snag the best parking space, and look like a model doing it.

He's wearing black jeans, chunky motorcycle boots, and a padded jacket that, once his helmet is stowed, gets peeled off like a second skin, leaving him in a black T-shirt. The all-black ensemble looks ridiculously good on him. I'm about to fan myself, and not because of the July midday sun. Then I see he's not alone. A leggy girl with pale skin and a cute pixie haircut is a couple of feet away, talking with a wide smile. She has black painted fingernails and in her strapless black sundress, she and Oliver look like a matched set. I couldn't feel frumpier in my unsophisticated boyfriend jeans and striped boatneck tee.

I'm too far away to hear their conversation, but they certainly seem to know each other. Oliver says something and the girl touches him lightly on the shoulder. Ugh. The universal symbol for "I'm reminding you that I'm available and interested in you." I slow my walk, not wanting to interrupt whatever this is.

No matter how heavily I drag my sneakered feet, she's still there when I get to the café. It would be highly immature to walk by without acknowledging them, even though part of me longs to just head inside.

Oliver solves the problem for me by exclaiming, "Kate!" when he sees me. "How are you?"

"Fine." I glance at the woman who gives me a friendly smile.

"Hi, I'm Ruby."

I smile back and hope I look normal. I note a SSDGM tattoo on her slender bicep. Dammit. She must be a fan of *My Favorite Murder*, one of my favorite podcasts. I don't want to like the pretty Murderino who feels free to touch my...nothing. Oliver's nothing. He's barely a friend. I shake it off. "See you inside?"

"I'm ready now," Oliver says quickly. "Nice to see you, Ruby."

"See ya, Oliver." Her eyes dart to me curiously, but she doesn't say anything else. Then she heads down the street toward the L.A. River.

"Friend?" I ask, hating myself for it.

"Yeah. Sort of."

With what womanly intuition I possess I'm certain they slept together. It doesn't matter if they did it last night or two months ago or two years ago. Los Angeles is probably littered with cool, podcast-loving girls who've slept with Oliver Mercier. I'm not special.

The night of the wedding he told me he was a player. I'm the living proof. And I refuse to be the reason for his life to change against his will. I refuse to be resented for wanting this baby. I square my shoulders. We're having lunch and we're not going to let this complication tie us up into any more knots than we have to.

CHAPTER 27

OLIVER

Inside the café I order a portobello mushroom sandwich and Kate orders a grilled cheese and a lemonade, protesting when I tap my credit card before she has a chance to wrangle hers out of her purse.

"You can get the next one," I say. "You want to sit inside?"

She frowns. "Outside."

It's blazing hot, but I shrug and hold the door open for her. We claim an umbrella-shaded table, the noise of the Los Feliz Boulevard traffic filling the silence between us. Kate doesn't seem in the mood for chitchat and I'm a little embarrassed about running into Ruby. She's a friend of a friend—we hooked up on and off for a while last year. Running into her today was random, but not entirely unwelcome. We parted on good terms, and her attitude today made it clear she wouldn't mind starting up again.

A month ago, I would have seriously considered it. Now the idea of pursuing any woman other than the one sitting across from me makes me feel like I'm struggling to put on someone else's bespoke suit. It's not a good fit.

Speaking of fitting, Kate is dressed casually today, her cheeks flushed from the summer heat. It's only been a few days since I've seen her, but she looks lovelier than ever and ripe as a peach.

The only thing on my mind should be the monumental thing we're facing together, but the fact is I want to kiss Kate so badly I can practically taste her. It's hard to care about anything else.

"So, that's the infamous motorcycle, huh?" She gestures to my bike, gleaming a few feet away in the sun.

"Yep. It's a hot day to ride, but the SUV's getting a brake job."

"Ah." She wraps her pink lips around a paper straw. The wanting to kiss her thing gets worse.

"I told my family about the baby."

I concentrate on her announcement instead of her mouth. "Oh, great. Right? I mean, was it great?"

She screws up her face. "It was okay. They're happy about the baby, as I predicted. But they're not quite sure what to make of you. Of us."

Same. "What did you tell them?"

"I told them we were friends who had a night together and are going to raise the baby together. I mean, not together-together, just, you know, on the same page."

"Oh." Well, that's accurate. But I'm still bereft at the casual assumption that we're in this together but only as far as the baby is concerned.

"Is that okay?"

"Sure. I mean, we're friends." I force the completely inadequate word through my teeth.

"Yeah. Yes. We are." She seems relieved, which raises my hackles. "How's everything with the restaurant? Still on schedule?"

"It's been hectic, but we're on target. Soft opening a week from today."

"Good luck, Oliver. I'm sure it's going to be a success."

"Yeah, thanks." A server brings us our order. Everything looks delicious, but this is far more important than lunch. "You have to be there."

"At the opening?" She takes a bite of her grilled cheese, doesn't look at me.

"Of course. I want you to be there. Please say you'll come. Please."

"I don't know—"

"Ricky and Nicole are coming. You can invite whoever else you want—let me know how many people and I'll add them to the list."

"I don't think—"

Her hesitation grates on me, abrading the protective shell I've been trying to keep over my heart. I haven't wanted to upset our precarious balance, but I'm tired of being careful. I reach across the table, sweep up her hands in mine. "Kate, look at me."

She moves her head; her stricken expression turns my stomach. I'm sickly certain everything is about to go sideways. Still, I have to try.

"I don't know why you're pretending like we're barely acquaintances who are only interacting because of one night that went in a direction neither of us planned on, but please, stop it. We mean more to each other than that. I don't want to be just your friend."

"Oliver, I—" I know she's going to deny me, so I plow on, not letting her break my heart. Not just yet.

"I haven't known you very long, but sometimes you just know what you want. I want you, Kate. We're good together, aren't we? Since the wedding I've been trying to give you space, but that's dumb. I don't want space. I want to be with you."

I steel myself for her to run away, to bolt like she's done every other time I've gotten too close to her. She's not hightailing it out of here, so I brush my thumbs over her knuckles, a tiny tendril of hope working through my chest.

"When you told me we were going to be parents, I was hell-bent on you giving me a chance to prove to you I could be a good partner, a good dad. It didn't take me long to realize I wanted you to give me a chance to be a different kind of partner. That's all I want, a chance. Can I have that?"

Her wide eyes are dry, but suddenly she's breathing in hitches and gulps like she's crying all the same. My own breath catches in apprehension.

"Sweetheart? Kate? Oh no, are you having a panic attack?"

She nods jerkily, her breathing shallow. "Shit." I jump out of my chair, move to her side, rub circles on her back. "I'm sorry. Fuck. Should I call someone?"

She shakes her head, grabs some water, takes a shaky sip. I keep rubbing her back, oblivious to anything except the rise and fall of her shoulders, the color in her cheeks, and the extreme relief I experience when she slowly gets her breathing under control and sits up straight. I sink back to kneel beside her.

"I'm sorry, sweetheart. I guess you weren't expecting that."

She laughs without mirth. "Oliver, you have never been what I expected, not from the moment I met you."

"I'm sorry," I say again, uselessly.

"I'm sorry, too," she whispers. "I can't do that. I can't do what you're asking. I'm strong, but I'm not strong enough for that."

"You don't have to be strong all the time. You can let me take some of the burden for you."

"That's not what I do."

"Try it. Please."

She takes a breath, reassuringly deep and steady, and looks me right in the eye. "No."

Well, that's pretty definitive. I stiffen with disappointment, that tendril of hope dead and ground into dust. "Okay. I get it."

"Look, I don't blame you if I think I'm a nutcase. I've been all over the place lately, and I can only blame that partly on these stupid hormones. I've sent mixed messages, but you can't honestly expect me to jump into a relationship with you two minutes after some girl was hanging all over you, when you drive a vehicle that could turn you into roadkill in the blink of an eye, when you've never had a long-term relationship before. You say you want this baby, and you've been really good to me, but your entire life is about to change and I don't think you've considered exactly what that means. You work night and day now, right? Well, your time won't be your own anymore. You can't take a baby on a motorcycle. And I could be wrong, but it could put a serious crimp in your game."

The bike, the girls, work. Those are details I can fix. Kate's the one I can't live without. "You aren't listening to me. I don't want anyone else. I want you."

"Well, maybe these crazy-making baby hormones are catching, because you don't know me."

I'm too stunned to respond.

"You're in love with a fantasy that we're going to make a big happy family. But as much as I like you, Oliver, that's something I can't give you."

I finally get it—she doesn't want me like I want her. Though I feel a little like I'm drowning and falling off a cliff at the same time, I'll deal with my feelings later. Kate's face is red with emotion and I'm worried she'll get heat stroke. I need to make sure she's okay.

"I'm sorry I upset you. Look, I'll drive you back to work. We can take your car and I'll Uber back here." I flag down a passing server and ask for to-go boxes for our food.

"It's okay. I'm fine to drive."

"Let me. Please." I've never begged a woman for anything in my life.

"Oliver. I don't need your help." Her voice is hard like the pavement under my knees, with as little give.

I rise, feeling creaky. Careening off my bike at top speed might feel something close to how crushed I am.

"You don't want me, fine. You don't want my help, okay. But I am going to be a part of your life, Kate. And I need you to let me be there for you, and for our baby." I hand her both boxes of leftovers, my own appetite having vanished along with my hope. "Have a good day at work."

I manage to put on my helmet and get my bike on the road without embarrassing myself. I don't look back.

CHAPTER 28
KATE

KATE

You've got to tell me I'm doing the right thing.

You're doing the right thing.

About what?

About Oliver. He told me he wants to be
with me.

And you said???

I said no, obviously

Oh

What does that mean?

Nothing. You're doing the right thing.

OK, that's what I thought.

Is it?

'Cause I think you want it to be the right thing,
maybe think it's the right thing. Maybe it even
feels like the right thing.

But you've been wrong before. You could be
wrong about this.

> I thought you'd back me up on this. The other
> girls are biased. My mom and sister are almost
> worse than Nicole. Why can't anyone accept
> that maybe I want to be alone?

Kate, you've been alone for a long time. You
wanted to be alone and you were. In a few
months, you're never going to be alone again.
That's scary. Oliver might not be the guy for
you. Maybe there is no guy for you.

But don't confuse wanting to be alone with
being afraid. Remember how you texted me a
few weeks ago because that guy asked you to
dinner and you said no but you kinda wanted
to say yes?

What happened to that Kate? The one who
thought maybe she was ready? 'Cause it
sounds like maybe you're just scared that
Oliver wasn't who you thought he was. You
thought he was a hot one-night stand and now
it turns out he's a hot guy who's offering you
something infinitely scarier. A family. A future.
Now, if you think that brewery guy is hotter
than Oliver and you'd rather date him, go for it.
If you want to stay home every night from now
until eternity raising your kid on your own, I'll
support you. But if you really thought you'd
done the right thing by turning Oliver down
you wouldn't have texted me.

You already know what you want. Stop being
afraid and just go for it.

> Are you done?

Um, yes

Do you hate me now?

No

So you going to ask brewery guy out?

No

You think I'd like him?

😈 I'll find his number.

Nah, that's OK. What about Oliver?

I don't know. But thanks. That's why I texted you. I knew you'd give me the truth, whether I want to hear it or not.

At your service.

Love you.

You do?

Yeah.

Well, I guess I love you, too.

🩶

* * *

NICOLE

We're home! Paris was bliss, but I'm seriously jet-lagged. Call you tomorrow.

KATE

Welcome home!

Can't wait to hear everything I missed! Let's schedule a wedding debrief soon.

* * *

KATE

> Red alert: Nicole's back and she wants to
> debrief.

LANI

O, aren't you and your boy going to Bali soon?

O

Thursday

LANI

Let's use that as an excuse to put it off. Not
that I don't want to see you all. I'm just still in
wedding detox mode.

ROSIE

Me too. My feet still hurt.

LANI

It's been three weeks!

ROSIE

I'm never wearing 4 inch heels again, I don't
care who gets married.

> Nobody's getting married. Read the fine print
> of this group.

ROSIE

Oh right.

O

Well, I'll tell her I'm too busy with trip prep.

LANI

Thanks O. I owe you.

> We'll all get together soon, with as little
> wedding chat as possible.

ROSIE

Sounds good. Kisses! Gotta run. I'm
babysitting for Jake & Becca.

O

Have fun/good luck.

ROSIE

Don't worry, Gus is coming, too.

LANI

You know if you & Gus weren't together you
could figure it out on your own, right?

ROSIE

Of course I could. But I don't have to. It's nice.

LANI

I give up. And I'm going to the Bowl to see The
Flaming Lips.

O

Alone?

LANI

With a very nice man I met at the bank. Who
has Flaming Lips tickets.

Enjoy. Be safe.

LANI

Don't worry, I'm driving myself, I won't take
drinks from anyone, and I have my pepper
spray on my keychain. And I'll text when I get
home.

Ah, the joys of dating in the 21st century.

O

You see why I opted out?

LANI

Until you realized you already had a platonic
life partner you secretly wanted to bone.

O

It wasn't a perfect system.

LANI

Whatever—see ya xoxo

> Be good. I'm going to take a bath, aka the last bastion of pregnant lady indulgences.

O

Ooh, a bath sounds great. That's one reason to move in with Jamie—he has an awesome bathtub and I only have my tiny little shower.

> Are you thinking about moving in?!

O

We've talked about it. We're going to revisit after Bali.

> Sounds great. You guys are really made for each other.

O

I know, it's kind of embarrassing.

> Don't be like that. I'm happy for you.

O

Thanks. I'm happy, too.

> That's all that matters.

If only I could take my own advice.

CHAPTER 29

OLIVER

I f leaving Kate behind at the café yesterday was difficult, it's
nothing compared to waking up Saturday morning to the
knowledge I have to face the rest of my life without her.

Of course I'll see her often in the coming weeks, months,
years. Will it hurt every time? One day will she meet someone
she's not afraid to try with? Will I have to watch her make a life
with someone else?

If the restaurant weren't opening in six days, I would have
pulled the covers over my head and gone back to sleep. At it is,
I'm groggy and grumpy when I pull up to Mercy SB a couple of
hours later. Jamila's car is there, and a few others I don't recognize, presumably kitchen staff who are training. I've brought a
few folks from the original Mercy kitchen to help with the
opening, but the menu has so many new dishes, everyone's got
a steep learning curve.

I spend time in the office going over the paperwork for
Jamila's recent hires and conferencing with my general
manager over the plans for opening night. I'm inspecting the
recently installed bag hooks under the bar when Ricky Kendell
strolls in, looking tanned and relaxed in chinos, loafers, and a
blue oxford shirt unbuttoned at the collar.

"Ricky, this is an unexpected pleasure," I say, because what else can you say when your most important investor arrives unannounced six days before opening? I haven't forgotten our last meeting, when he gave me the disturbing older-brother speech about Kate. I wonder if he's talked to her since yesterday. He might be here to check up on me just as much as the restaurant. "When did you get back? How was Paris?"

"Paris was awesome. I had never been before, so we tried to see everything. I actually slept the entire flight home. Being a tourist is exhausting."

"And how's your lovely bride?"

"Nicole is Nicole," he says, as if that explains everything, which it kind of does. "She got inspired by a bunch of the art we saw so she's been sketching new designs nonstop since we got back."

"That's great." I want to ask about Kate on the off chance he knows how she is. It's been hard to stop myself from texting her. I haven't quite figured out how to temper her unequivocal request for space with my need to take care of her.

Ricky looks around approvingly. "The space looks terrific, Oliver. It's even better than the spec drawings."

I breathe an internal sigh of relief. "We're really pleased with how it turned out. The indoor-outdoor space is going to be a really special amenity."

We talk shop for a while, and I'm pleased with how enthusiastically he reacts to all of my ideas and plans. He'd told me when we entered into this arrangement he'd be hands-off, that he trusted my vision and approved of it, but it's nice to see him stick to his word.

"You've got everything under control, Oliver. I can't wait until Friday."

I grimace. "I'm looking forward to Saturday more, to be honest. Opening night I tend to be a basket case."

"You're going to kill it. You've hired the best people, plus Nat won't let this place bow with anything less than a splash. Nicole and I will be here to toast to Mercy SB's success. We're bringing River and Liz, too."

"I'll make sure they're on the list." I pause. "Anyone else you're planning to invite? Any of Nicole's friends?"

He looks at me impassively. "Well, Ophelia and my cousin Jamie are heading out of town, so they won't be here, and I think Rosie and Gus have some family party to attend. I'll see if Nicole can get her business partner Lani to come. Why? You worried about numbers?"

"No, no, should be a full house," I say. If anything, we'll be pushing capacity. I swallow any pride I might have left. "What about Kate?"

He side-eyes me. "What about her?"

I might be flirting with disaster but instead of backing off I double down. "Look, I'm going to level with you. I—she—it's complicated. I invited her to the opening but I'm not sure she's going to come. I thought maybe if you invited her, she'd be more willing to be there."

"I'm sure I'm not telling you anything you don't know when I say no one can get Kate to do anything she doesn't want to."

"True." He hasn't given me much hope, but he hasn't pulled out the proverbial shotgun yet, either.

"Look, I know I haven't known her for very long, but I really care about her. She's keeping me at arm's length, which is her right, but I still need to know she's okay."

"Going around her back to get me to get her to come to the opening isn't supporting her, it's trying to manipulate the situation."

I consider this. "Fair. But what am I supposed to do, man? She won't let me do anything for her. It's so frustrating."

"There are more ways to a woman's heart than acts of service."

"I suppose I could send her flowers?"

"They'd have to be local, sustainable ones."

"Naturally."

I'm thinking hard when Ricky's stomach gurgles loudly. "I'm sorry, I'm distracting us both with my problems. It's lunchtime, you must be—" I stop. That's it. "Hang on—I'm going to send her lunch. She's not going to send away a food delivery person—that would be wasteful. And that way I can be sure she's eating at least one proper meal a day."

"Devious and thoughtful," Ricky says.

"What to get her? I know she likes cheeseburgers, but those don't travel well. What do you think? Falafel? Does she like Middle Eastern food?"

Ricky shakes his head. "No idea. I'll text Nicole to find out."

"Thanks. I'd hate to send her something she doesn't like."

I pull up the menu for my favorite falafel place on my phone while Ricky texts Nicole. A few minutes later, the verdict is in: Kate loves hummus and all things hummus-adjacent and I've got an order coming her way. I feel slightly more optimistic than I have in a while.

"Thanks for your help, Ricky. You're a good man."

He gives me a small smile. "I've known Kate as long as I've known Nicole. She's a dear friend, and she's been through a lot. If I didn't think you were good for her, believe me, I wouldn't be lifting a finger."

"Thanks, man."

"But just because you're buying her lunch doesn't give you carte blanche to stalk her or anything."

I hold up my hands. "Of course not." Just then a clatter and a bunch of swear words come from the direction of the kitchen. We turn our heads sharply. I'm praying that whatever that was won't turn out to be a major catastrophe.

Ricky pats his stomach and grins, jerking his head toward the kitchen. "I'm starving. You got anything to eat around here?"

CHAPTER 30

KATE

The day after the unfortunate lunch at Village Bakery, I'm three freeways away at The Ripped Bodice. The clever name of the romance-only bookstore in Culver City reminds me of the night of Nicole's wedding, when Oliver helped me escape the confines of my bridesmaid dress.

He behaved like a gentleman that night. Except for a little harmless flirting, and the fact that we had sex after barely learning each other's names, he's always acted so proper around me. Even when he told me he had feelings for me and endured my shooting him down, he's never treated me with anything less than respect.

I may have been obsessing about Oliver for twenty-four hours, about what he'd said and what I could have done differently, but I'm on a different mission at the moment, looking for a birthday present for my sister.

Kelly loves romances, so I browse, slightly overwhelmed by the range of books on display. Not a regular romance reader myself, I'd been imagining a lot of paperbacks adorned by bare-chested men, but there's everything from dark covers with brooding, bearded heroes to brightly colored cartoon illustrated covers, doorstop historical epics to angst-ridden young adult fare. I doubt Kelly wants anything angsty, so I grab three cheerful-looking recommended new releases plus a reusable tote bag to use as wrapping paper. Voilà, birthday present solved.

My elation at having done something right for once is short-lived when I check my phone. I have a text from Nicole, and another from an unknown number. I read that one first: it's a notification that my lunch order from Falafel Queen is ready to be delivered and can I confirm the delivery address.

I almost ignore it as spam, but then I pause, and not just because falafel sounds delicious. I call the number in the text and learn that yes, an order had been placed for me that morning by a Mr. Mercer—I wince as they butcher Oliver's last name—and where do I want it to go? I give them my work address, hoping if I leave Culver City now I can beat the delivery person there.

As I battle Saturday traffic up Fairfax, my mind races. Oliver bought me lunch? That makes two days in a row. I'm partly annoyed at his high-handedness—what if I'd had other plans? But it's kind of sweet. He wants me to eat. He wants to make things easier for me. And since I'm not giving him much of an opportunity to do anything else, he's finding a way.

My Bluetooth rings while I'm waiting to turn onto Wilshire. I tap the button and Nicole's voice floods my tiny car.

"Hi! I'm back!"

"I know. How was the flight?"

I get the honeymoon travel download and by the time I'm turning onto Cahuenga, I feel like I was the one stuck on the runway for an hour waiting for a gate at LAX. I break into her monologue. "I'm almost at work, can we talk more later?"

"Sure, but wait—what about Oliver?"

My stomach dips and I have to slam on the brakes to avoid running a red light. I really shouldn't be talking and driving at the same time. "What?"

"Didn't you get my text? Did Oliver Mercier reach you?"

"Huh?"

"All I know is Ricky texted me to ask if you like hummus and I was like, who doesn't, and then I was like, why do you need to know, and he said he didn't need to know, Oliver needed to know, and so I told him to tell Oliver to ask you himself, but I figured I'd give you a heads-up. Anyway. I didn't know you knew each other. I only met him for the first time at the wedding."

I blink to clear my head and ease back onto the gas when the light changes to green.

"Yeah, um, about that. He sent me lunch from Falafel Queen, apparently."

"Random. What's going on, Kate?"

"Listen, I have to run to work. We'll talk soon, okay?"

"But—"

I cut her off mid-sentence, driving the rest of the way with my hands in a white-knuckle grip on my steering wheel, stopping at every yellow light and driving exactly the speed limit.

The office is deserted when I arrive, except for a delivery gal who hands me a giant bag of food, enough for five people. She waves away the bill I offer her, saying the tip has been taken care of.

I make myself a falafel feast in the office kitchenette that normally smells of instant coffee and slightly sour milk. No one else is here; it's just me and my lunch. The lunch Oliver bought for me. Not just bought. Arranged. Conceived. Executed. That's what he does. He has ideas and then he figures out how to make them happen, or hires the right people to make them happen for him.

The cynical, brittle part of me argues that Oliver sees me as a problem to solve. He probably asked someone who works for him to order the food. Then again, he talked to Ricky to find out what I like. He didn't hand this off to an assistant.

So if I'm not a problem for Oliver to solve, what am I? The woman who changed the course of his life, sure. But is he imagining a deeper connection between us? Is that why he wants to pursue more than a practical partnership with me? Because it makes a certain kind of sense on paper, or because this is how we're supposed to be, baby or no baby?

The building is so quiet I notice my own eating sounds. Once I hear myself chewing, I can't un-hear it. I swallow the last bite of tender falafel hastily. If I were eating with Oliver, I wouldn't be having misophonia. We'd be talking and laughing and maybe discussing baby names or the last-minute problems at the restaurant or the new podcast I'm in preproduction on. We'd share lunch, and then we'd share a kiss when he left to go back to work. If we lived together, we'd share dinner and a bed.

We'd share our lives.

I shiver. In fear? In hope? Perhaps you can't have one without the other, not when you know what it's like to lose.

The look in Oliver's eyes yesterday when he was virtually begging me to give him a chance haunts me. I'm starting to desperately want to give him that.

My fingers itch with wanting to call Oliver and thank him for the food, for taking care of me even when I'm ungrateful and difficult and skittish and—

Enough.

Instead of calling him, I scroll through my contact list. The Never a Brides have had enough of my complaining. Nicole doesn't even know that Oliver's the father of the bun in my oven. My mom's hardly objective, and Kelly's worse. I have so many people in my life who care about me and who want me to be happy. I'm so lucky, in so many ways.

I know what I want to do, and I know who I need to call.

I hit his name before I can chicken out. The phone rings three agonizingly slow times before he picks up.

"Kate? Everything okay?" Ricky's voice is calm but with an

overlay of concern, which is understandable since it's possible I've never actually called him on the phone in the entire decade-plus we've known each other.

"Yes, everything's okay, I just need to talk to you for a minute."

"Sure. What's up?" He's making an effort to not make this awkward, which I appreciate.

On a whoosh of air, I start talking and hope he can keep up. "I'm not sure if you know this or not—at this point I can't really keep track of who knows what—but Oliver Mercier is the guy I'm having this baby with. I told him at your wedding—I hadn't even known how to contact him and there he was, like magic, at your stupid wedding—not that your wedding was stupid, but it's just, I wasn't expecting it. Story of my life, really, but the reason I'm calling is because Oliver...wants to be with me. Which is crazy, right? I mean, how can you fall for someone that fast? But the thing is, I think it's happening to me, too, even though I sent him away, but he's still trying to take care of me without being overbearing about it. Anyway, that's the reason I'm calling."

There's a pause, as if Ricky's waiting to make sure I'm done spewing into his ear. "I'm sorry, what's the reason you're calling?"

I grit my teeth and try again.

"You said Ben would be proud of me, that he'd be happy for me. You knew him, and I need to know what you think he would have thought about all of this. We did everything so conventionally—we dated for months before we even had sex. It was all so by the book, until he died and I lost the plot." My voice has gone wistful.

Ricky clears his throat. "If you're asking me if I think Ben would approve of you and Oliver seeing if you could have a future together, the answer is yes. Oliver's good people, Kate. He's a hell of a businessman, and he's great to his employees.

He gives a percentage of his profits to charity and he runs a sustainable business. That's why I chose to invest in his restaurant. But you don't need me to give you permission, and you don't need Ben to give you permission. You have to give yourself permission. Can you do that?"

"I don't know." I sigh. "I'd like to try. I just feel like maybe I'll be healthier if I let myself be less strong. That it's time for me to be less afraid. Is that crazy?"

"You deserve a little crazy. You deserve something good. If Oliver could be good for you, then that's all the answer you need."

"And it's not super weird that we're doing everything out of order?"

"Fuck the order."

I'm shocked. I could probably count the number of times I've heard him say fuck on, well, one finger.

"Fuck convention. Fuck everybody else and their expectations."

Jesus, three fingers and counting.

"Seriously? You and Nicole have done everything that everyone expected of you since forever."

He laughs humorlessly. "You know when I knew that Nicole was going to be the person I'd spend the rest of my life with?"

"When?"

"First semester of freshman year, first day of Econ 101. I saw this vivacious blonde laughing with a cute redhead and I got this weird feeling in my gut—a feeling I've had a few times since, usually regarding stocks that are about to split—and I knew that woman was going to be my future."

I'm flabbergasted. "Freshman year? But you guys didn't start dating until the end of junior year."

"Exactly. Despite what it looks like from the outside, our relationship hasn't been one smooth crescendo 'til death do us part. So if Oliver says he fell that fast, I believe him. After all, if I were partial to redheads, then Nicole's cute friend might have been the object of my affections instead."

"What?" I yelp. "I was the cute redhead from your story?"

He chuckles. "You're still pretty cute, Kate."

"Wow. You've certainly given me plenty to think about in a squicky *Sliding Doors*-esque way. Maybe this is how it was supposed to happen all along."

"And maybe you should stop overthinking it and do what feels good."

What feels good? Eating falafel would have felt a lot better if Oliver were here. Kissing him, being intimate with him, is the best I've felt in literally years. And aside from those fleeting moments when I allowed myself to feel pleasure, I've pushed him away every chance I've gotten.

"Thanks for the pep talk, Coach." I review my options. I'm going to need help if I'm going to turn this ship around. "Are you going to the opening of Mercy SB?"

"Of course. The question is, are you going to be there?"

"With bells on."

* * *

That night after work, I stretch out in my bathtub and type out a careful text.

> Thank you for lunch. It was delicious. It reminded me of a foodie podcast called Midnight Falafel. You might want to give it a listen.

I'm toweling off when I get his reply.

> I'll definitely check it out. Goodnight, Kate.

"Goodnight," I say to my empty room.

CHAPTER 31

KATE

S unday Oliver sends me French food and I send Oliver a French podcast about food.

Monday it's green juice and doughnuts. They balance each other out. I send him the "Searching for the Donut King" episode of *Sporkful*.

Tuesday I send him my favorite episode of *My Favorite Murder*, the one about the eccentric coconut-obsessed guy who made his wife pull out all her teeth and go live on a tropical island. Oliver sends me a series of incredulous texts as he listens, and I laugh at every single one. He sends me vegetarian sushi and a tray of mochi. I'm not ashamed to say I eat the entire tray while binging Marie Kondo. Being pregnant has its perks.

Wednesday and Thursday are more of the same—thoughtful gifts of food from Oliver, and me trying to match with on-topic podcasts. I haven't had to go grocery shopping in a week, and my fridge is full of fragrant leftovers. I wonder if dating a restaurateur means never having to cook again. That's almost enough to have me picking up the phone and texting him *let's do this*.

But I'm not so much of a coward that I'll enter into a relationship via text.

The other exciting thing that happens is I call Darsh, the son of my parents' neighbor, and find out he's just graduated from UCLA with a degree in communications, is a huge fan of *Brew O'Clock*, and is looking for a job. I consider hiring him over the phone, but invite him to come to the studio for a proper interview like the bona fide businesswoman I am.

Darsh arrives at the studio Thursday morning, a twenty-two-year-old's version of dressed up in slacks and a button-down shirt, which shows me he's taking this opportunity seriously. Slacks instead of jeans is practically wearing a tuxedo in Los Angeles.

I promise him I'll never ask him to pick up my dry cleaning but I might ask him to buy coffee. He says he's happy to pick up dry cleaning as long as I expose him to the technical side of the business as well as the administrative side. Since having an experienced right-hand man is going to come in handy once I become a mom—crying babies and podcast tapings don't mix, I can already tell—I agree to his terms. We negotiate a month-long trial period and he says he can start right away.

His first act as my assistant is canceling the green smoothie subscription I haven't had the heart to. I've finally accepted that these punitively healthy drinks don't make me miss Ben less, and not drinking them won't cause me to forget him faster. Darsh's second task is fielding a call from my OB's office. He holds out the phone. "It's Dr. Sorensen?"

"Oh, thanks, I'll take that," I say. "Maybe you can, um, familiarize yourself with the studios? I think Jay's in B. Tell him I want him to give you a tour."

"You got it." And out saunters my brand-new assistant.

Without ceremony, Dr. Sorensen announces, "Oliver Mercier is the father of your baby. Are you ready to hear the sex?"

"Oh. Yeah. Have you told him?"

"He's next on my list to call."

"Okay."

"You are having a boy."

I let out a little squeak and tears spring to my eyes. I'm reasonably sure my reaction would be the same no matter if she'd said boy, girl, or none of the above, but it's still exciting. It makes the whole thing slightly easier to wrap my brain around. I pat my growing tummy. Me and my boy. We're in this together.

"Thanks, Dr. Sorensen."

"See you in a few weeks."

Should I call Oliver? He's going to be as awed as I am, I predict. But he's also super busy with tomorrow night's opening. I'm sure he's in the middle of a million things getting ready, and I don't want to bother him.

I'm also a huge coward, and it's taking all of my courage to go through with my plan as it is.

I avoid texting the Never a Brides, worried they'll talk me out of it, and I definitely don't call Nicole, whose emotional bombs I can't handle right now. But, late that night when I'm done taping and exhausted from training Darsh, I call my mom.

"Everything okay, Kate?"

"Yeah, everything's good." I'm sitting on my couch, rubbing my feet, contemplating yet another bath. "I just wanted to tell you I hired Darsh on a trial basis today, and so far he's a rock star. Thanks for the recommendation."

"That's fantastic. I'm so happy you're going to have someone to help you. You're growing your business, so you need to grow your staff, too."

"You're right. There's something else—I heard from the doctor today and I'm having a boy."

"Oh!" She makes the same squeaky mouse noise that I did

when I found out and I smile. "A boy. Riley's going to have so much fun with a baby boy cousin."

"Awesome." I smile at the thought of Riley and her cousin chasing each other around my parents' yard, the way Kelly and I did when we were little.

"Is Oliver excited?"

"Um. I'm not sure. I haven't talked to him since I found out. He's opening a new restaurant tomorrow and he's slammed. But I'm sure he'll be delighted."

"I hope we get to meet him soon," Mom says carefully.

"Yeah, um, I want to clear up something about Oliver. I know I said we're friends and we had a night together, and that's technically true, but it happened the other way around. We met at a club and I spent the night with him, and then I didn't see him again for two months, when I told him I was pregnant."

"Sweetie, wow." She doesn't sound judgmental. If anything, she sounds a little impressed.

"Since then we really have become friends. And more than that. I have feelings for him. And I think he feels the same way." Oliver hasn't technically rescinded his declaration of wanting to be with me, but I have no idea if that's still on the table.

"If he has eyes in his head, I'm sure he's head over heels for you."

"Thanks, Mom. I just wanted to tell you that whatever happens with Oliver, I think I understand what you were trying to tell me before. It's been, well, it's been a long road to get here, and I appreciate that you didn't give up on me, that you encouraged me not to give up on life. You were right."

"Sweetie." She doesn't say anything else, and I'm pretty sure she's trying not to cry.

"I love you."

"Love you, too," she says quickly, voice husky.

We get back to normal by discussing the latest adorable

thing Riley did, and bandy around ideas for a baby shower down the line. "You know what, you and Nicole should coordinate on that. Something tells me she's going to want in."

"You want me and Nicole to work together to plan your baby shower?" Mom's voice is incredulous. "What have I done to deserve that?"

"She's not that bad," I protest. "Okay, maybe she is. Tell you what, you can do a family party and she can do the friends one."

"Deal."

I'm feeling unusually centered by the time I sink into my now-ritual nightly bath. This baby and I have a lot of people who love and care about us, and I don't always have to do everything all by myself. I'm growing, literally and emotionally. It doesn't matter if I'm still figuring out my own feelings, or if maybe Oliver and I are confusing lust and circumstances with true love. What we have feels like the start of something real, and I have to try. And either way, I believe I'll be okay.

CHAPTER 32

OLIVER

Mercy SB's opening day finds me so jittery I'm making myself sick. There are literally a thousand different things that could go wrong—and some of them absolutely will. It's my third time doing this. You'd think I'd be used to the nerves.

"Take a chill pill, boss," Nat says when I try to take a sip of coffee, type a text, and bark at a server who is setting water glasses too close to the wine glasses all at the same time, resulting in coffee spilling all over my shirt *and* my phone. The server hightails it to the kitchen.

"Chill is the last thing I need. More coffee." I wave my now-empty mug in her direction pathetically.

"You can have more coffee after I see you eat something that doesn't contain sugar."

I might have overdone it with the pastry order this morning. I lost count at my third pain au chocolat and my stomach feels queasy. I can't argue successfully with her when I'm at the top of my game, so in my current condition, I'm doomed.

"Fine. What should I eat?"

"Go get some tamales from the food truck on the corner and let me deal with this inexcusable water glass situation."

She shoos me out of my own restaurant, and since I might go insane if I don't get out of my head for a minute, I don't bother arguing.

There's a line at the food truck, but it feels good to be outside. It's late July, but this part of town never gets unbearably hot. Palm trees wave lazily in the breeze coming off the water. It's that in-between time when it's too late for lunch and too early for dinner, when the State Street shoppers' feet start dragging and the young people begin gearing up for their nighttime plans. The traffic picks up in the Funk Zone as people of all ages celebrate the end of the week by imbibing a beer or two.

I order two pork tamales and eat them standing up on the corner as I mentally talk myself down. The coffee on my shirt dries stiff, but no matter, I have an entirely different outfit to change into later. Nat will put the fear of god into the servers if I haven't already accomplished that. It's not even going to be a tough crowd. Tonight's guest list is mainly comprised of friendly faces who are there to celebrate. Tomorrow night will be the first time we're open to the public, to the critics, to the Yelp reviewers, to the Instagram influencers who'll be taking pictures of everything on the menu and passing judgment.

Still, my restaurants are like my children and I want each one to get off to the best possible start. I can only hope the hours upon hours of work I've put in will pay off.

I see a woman with red hair walking up the block and think of Kate. I've asked her a couple of times in our recent text exchanges if she's coming tonight and gotten noncommittal replies. It's peculiar—I shouldn't want the added stress of navigating our tricky relationship, but somehow it won't feel right if she's not there. She's become such an important part of my life in such a short amount of time.

I tell myself that if she's not there, it's because she doesn't want to distract me, doesn't want to impose, not because she doesn't care about me. I'm coming to terms with the fact that she may never care about me as intensely, as passionately, as I care about her, but it's still painful. Will this low-level grief ever go away, or will it be a fresh hurt every time I see her, like scraping at a scab so that it can never fully heal?

After the last bite I'm calmer. Goddammit, is Nat *always* right? I walk slowly back to the front of Mercy SB and pause, taking it all in.

The building is handsome, the lines of the original warehouse still visible, but with reclaimed wood features added, like sliding windows that allow the front to be completely open to the street. One of the perks of Southern California life is the bleeding together of indoor and outdoor space. The dining room is just dark enough to feel intimate, but the warm glow of the industrial lighting makes the atmosphere cozy.

Everything is as it should be. We're ready. All Mercy SB needs now is people to bring it to life, to set into motion everything my team has worked so hard to achieve over these past months. We've built something special, something that's going to bring joy to people, something that's going to last. Something I can be proud of.

I nod. I am proud of this. So what if Kate doesn't come, or my parents aren't impressed, or the critics hate the Moroccan-influenced menu. I brought this into being, and it's going to be fucking awesome.

With that, I go inside to change my clothes in order to complete my transformation into Oliver Mercier, restaurant owner extraordinaire.

* * *

Three hours later the house is full—everyone who's on the list has shown up, and more. Ricky and Nicole are at a corner table with River and their partner, Liz. The photographer I met at the wedding is flitting about, doing her thing. A few minor investors are holding court at the bar, well lubricated and laughing, and it's only just six.

Everyone seems satisfied, and I've greeted nearly every single person by name, with a little help from Nat, of course. She's been running the front of the house, while I switch back and forth to the kitchen, making sure Jamila and her crew have everything they need.

I stick my head back there and survey the controlled chaos. The air is hot and smells like roasting meat. The line cooks have sweaty foreheads and occasionally shout something in their special restaurant code, but there's only a sense of very intense concentration, not of panic, so I calm down slightly.

"How's it going out there, Oliver?" Jamila, in chef's whites, calls out to me.

"So far, so good." I don't want to jinx it. "You're going to have to find a few minutes to come meet some people."

"Let me get through this rush," she says. "I need this re-plated, Anita. Fire the lamb, Jorge." I've been dismissed.

When I return to the dining room, the volume has risen slightly, which is good. Noise tends to correlate with people enjoying themselves. Nat's crimson dress at the host stand catches my eye—she's hugging someone who looks a lot like my mom. I do a double take. It *is* my mom, effortlessly chic in a white shift dress that shows off her deep golden skin, dotted with her signature moles. She's not alone.

"Papa?"

I haven't seen my father in person in two years, but he looks the same, if grayer. He's not a tall man—I've got a few inches on him—but he has the bearing of an aristocrat, though his blood is decidedly proletariat. He's wearing a suit, of course, as he has nearly every day I can remember, and he's not smiling.

"Son," he says, a little stiff.

I turn to greet my mother with a hug and two cheek kisses,

her familiar perfume instantly enveloping me in a feeling of love and security.

"Olivier, darling, don't be mad," she says, her accent barely noticeable after so many years in the States.

"Why would I be mad, Maman?" I'm suddenly, strikingly grateful that they're here—both of them. I shake my father's hand. My smile seems to put him at ease, because he pulls me in for a half-hug before letting me go.

"You know I wasn't going to come until closer to my birthday, but I just couldn't wait to see your magnificent new restaurant. And your father's schedule happened to open up." She glances at him under extravagantly shadowed eyelids, and I'm positive she had something to do with rearranging his calendar. "We decided to come early. Nat said you wouldn't mind."

"Nat knew about this?"

"I know everything," she whispers terrifyingly in my ear, then to my parents in a normal voice says, "We're so honored to have you here. Please, allow me to show you to your table."

"I was wondering who we were saving 17 for," I say to no one in particular as she steers my parents to a nice table with a view of the side garden. I see them settled, ask my most experienced server to take care of them, and bring them the wine list myself.

It's not a long list, but it's been carefully curated by my sommelier and myself. I don't realize I'm holding my breath until my father has a chance to read through it and hums.

"Interesting," he says, and I start to breathe again. *Interesting* is a good thing when it comes to wine and my father.

"Mostly California, as you can see," I say. "But there are a few surprises on there."

"The pinot—that's intriguing." He taps the menu with tapered fingers.

Intriguing. Even better than interesting.

"I hope your distributor gave you a good price," he says sternly.

I hold back a laugh. "Bien sûr, Papa. Shall I bring you a bottle?"

"Well, I for one would like something with bubbles," Maman says, putting a hand on my cheek. "We are celebrating, after all. I'm so proud of you, Olivier." Her use of my real name makes my throat feel unaccountably thick. Somehow their being here feels like a collision of two worlds—the one I grew up in and wanted to escape from, and the one I built here that ended up being my own version of the same world. Here I'm always Oliver, but I never really stopped being Olivier, not to them, and not to myself.

"Thanks, Maman. And you can have anything you want, especially bubbles."

I busy myself at the bar, making sure the bottle of Roederer that I pick out for my mother is properly uncorked, and that the pinot noir for my father is the correct vintage. My sommelier could have done it, but I need the space to collect myself.

But it doesn't matter how calm and collected I think I am when I turn back to the dining room and see who walks through the door.

Kate's standing there, tall and strong and so beautiful it hurts, and just like that, my opening day jitters return full force.

I don't have chill when it comes to her.

CHAPTER 33

KATE

When I get to Mercy SB the first person I see is Oliver. He's at the edge of the bar, a bottle of wine in each hand, looking at me like I'm the best-slash-worst thing that's ever happened to him.

Sounds about right.

I smile, or try to, and wave, stupidly. He nods, but walks away, bringing the wine to a table near the patio. Perhaps my idea to surprise him at his big opening was ill-conceived. He doesn't need a distraction on this of all days. But he'd been so persistent in asking if I'd come, I didn't want to disappoint him.

I smooth my skirt nervously as I glance around the dining room. It's stunning, perfectly lit, almost every table full. The servers move around as if following intricate choreography. The air smells of spices and wine. I'm suddenly starving.

My gaze catches on someone frantically waving in a corner. It's Nicole impersonating a traffic controller, desperately trying to get me to come over. I hold up a hand to keep her at bay, my eyes seeking out Oliver on the other side of the room. He's pouring red wine for a handsome older gentleman who's outclassing every other dude in the joint in his linen suit. With a start, I recognize that strong jawline, the mischievous smile as he tastes his wine and nods his approval. That must be Oliver's dad. Jesus. That makes the woman sitting across from him Oliver's mom, aka Aziza, aka one of the first true supermodels. She's as exquisite as her pictures. She's dressed in a white shift that's simple but not plain. A diamond winks on her ring finger, but other than that, she's not dripping in jewels or anything.

She's not royalty, I remind myself, only an ex-supermodel and the future grandmother of my kid.

"Can I help you?" A woman in a scarlet A-line dress with tightly coiled brown hair wrapped up in a multi-colored scarf looks at me pleasantly, but also as if she'll happily throw me out if I'm not on some pre-approved list.

"Hi, I'm Kate Treanor. Oliver invited me."

"Kate?" Her dark eyes widen behind her cat's-eye glasses. Her gaze never leaves my face but I still feel as if I'm under a microscope. "Of course. We weren't sure if you could make it. I'm Nat."

"Oh! Hi!" I smile. "I've heard a lot about you."

"I'll bet," she says dryly.

"Mostly about how he couldn't survive without you," I add, hoping it's not too late to win her over.

"Oh, well, that's true." Her feathers go down, and she casts a glance over her shoulder where Oliver's still talking with—oh God, his *parents*. Having to meet them is inevitable.

"I can set you up at the bar and let Oliver know you're here?"

"I think I'll join my friends for now, if that's okay? Ricky and um...all of them?"

"Sure." Nat seems relieved. "I'll find you another chair."

Ricky jumps up when I get to their table and gives me a hug. I'm reassured by the solidness of his grip. He's become my accidental confidant, and I'm really happy that he's here and rooting for me.

I get another hug from Nicole, looking glamorous in an

empire-waist maxi dress, her long blonde hair brushed straight, giving her a '70s vibe. Lani is sitting next to her, put together as ever and rocking her signature red lipstick. We blow ironic air kisses to each other as a server materializes with a chair. I sit down next to Ricky and across from River and Liz. I try not to look at Oliver every five seconds. He's sitting with his parents, his back to me, but I know he knows I'm here.

To take my mind off what I'm planning to say to him, I order a glass of water and half the items on the appetizer menu.

Ricky gives me an encouraging smile. "You talked to Oliver yet?"

"Not yet."

"I didn't know you were coming tonight," Nicole says.

"It was kind of a last-minute decision." I reach over to take a slice of bread out of the basket in the middle of the table, then take a second. "Hope no one minds if I bogart this bread. The baby's hungry."

Liz and River exchange surprised glances.

"You're pregnant?" River asks.

My mouth's full of bread so I nod.

"Congrats!" Liz adds.

I swallow and smile. "Thanks. It's good that it's summer, because I can't fit into a single pair of my pants anymore."

"We'll go shopping for maternity clothes," Nicole declares. In response to my groan she pouts. "Come on, it'll be fun!"

"Fun to spend money on clothes I'll only wear for a few months?"

"Just a couple of outfits. You have to have something to wear to work."

I sigh, because I know she's right.

"I can't believe Lani is the only one of my friends who actually enjoys shopping. The rest of you are hopeless."

"I know a really cute resale shop that has a lot of maternity clothes," Lani says. "I could stop by and pick out a few things for you."

I'm about to accept Lani's offer when I see Nicole's devastated expression. "Why don't the three of us go together?" I say instead, and Nicole instantly perks up.

Then the first of the appetizers hits the table, and I'm too busy chowing down to worry about maternity clothes or Oliver or his parents. How can I be anxious about the rest of my life when the most insanely delicious caramelized Brussels sprouts I've ever had are melting in my mouth?

"Good sprouts, right?" River says.

"Understatement," I say, though it comes out garbled because my mouth is full.

Everyone seems to be laughing at me, but I don't care. I'm so blissed out on the food, I don't see Oliver until it's too late. All of a sudden he's at my elbow and asking how everything is.

"I think Kate's in love with the Brussels sprouts," Nicole says.

I cringe at her choice of words, but Oliver just says, "That's good to hear." He kneels down next to me like a waiter at a family-friendly chain restaurant.

"Can I get you anything else?" he asks in a low voice. He looks wonderful and smells like spiced coffee. "Order anything you want, it's all on the house."

"Thanks." My appetite suddenly disappears. "The place is beautiful, Oliver."

He lights up. "Thanks. I'm pleased."

"You should be. Um, if you have time later, can we talk?"

"Sure, of course." He ducks his head, and his eyes are a little shy when he looks back up at me through his lashes. "My parents are here. I wasn't expecting them—they surprised me. Would you be up for meeting them later?"

I take a deep breath. "Do they know?"

"No, but I can tell them if you want me to. Or I can wait and we can tell them together."

"What do you think?"

"Whatever you want, Kate."

"You know what, can we talk first, the two of us, just for a minute?" I'm getting a touch panicky, but we need to hash out our shit before we complicate things with his parents.

"Of course." Oliver glances around the crowded restaurant. "We can go to the back office."

I stand up and catch Lani smirking. Ricky's smiling, too, but Nicole looks like she's been watching a telenovela unfold in front of her without subtitles.

"Ricky, please tell her and put her out of her misery."

"What is she talking about?" Nicole stage-whispers. Ricky puts a finger over her lips.

"I'll tell you in a minute, baby," I hear as I follow Oliver through the crowd to the back of the room. We go down the hallway I remember from the only other time I've been here, but instead of going to the kitchen, he leads me to a little office on the other side of the corridor. It's cool and empty and he shuts the door behind us, sealing us off from the world.

"Wow, privacy. Super," I say, rubbing my damp palms on my skirt. Thank God it's an absorbent material and not vegan leather or something.

"I'm so glad you came tonight." Oliver gestures to the single chair behind the small metal desk, but I hold my ground.

"Sorry I was so wishy-washy. It looks like it's going well."

"So far, so good. I might even get some sleep tonight."

I notice the slight shadows under his eyes for the first time. "You do look a little tired."

"It's been a big push to get here. Nat's been amazing."

"I finally got to meet the famous Nat."

"I hope she was nice to you."

"Nice enough." I wipe my palms on my skirt again, apparently a nervous habit I'm developing. "Listen, I'm procrastinating. I came here to tell you something. Or to ask you something. Or—"

"What is it, Kate?" He looks a little tense, like I'm about to deliver bad news.

"First, did you talk to the doctor?" I'm such a coward, dragging my heels since I already know what he's going to say.

"Yeah, she called me yesterday. It's official. I'm the dad. And I passed the other test, too."

"What other test?"

"I've got a clean bill of health."

"Oh, I forgot." I figured as much, but it's nice to know we're both healthy. "That's good news, but what I have to say isn't about that."

"Then what is it?"

"I don't know if you remember this, but at the wedding you asked me something. You asked why you, why I picked you, why I let you take me home."

He nods, looking puzzled.

"I never answered you, because I wasn't ready to tell you the truth. And I don't feel particularly ready now, but I'm more ready than I was and I think I could be even more ready if you give me a chance." God, I should have written something down, like a script. I close my eyes. Yeah, this is a gig. I'm giving lines. I can do that. I open my eyes, determined to do better.

"I picked you, not because I was drunk, though I wasn't exactly sober. And not because you were the hottest guy in the club, even though you were. I didn't set out to pick someone up or to get laid. But I wanted to feel...different. I wanted to know I could be someone different if I tried really hard. When I saw you, and I danced with you, you made it easy for me to be someone different. Someone with a life. I've spent so much of the last three years stuck in the past. Because of you, I finally get to move into the present. I got more than I bargained for because now we have to think about the future, too.

"I've been thinking about that future a lot over the last few days. I knew I wanted this baby. I had no idea I'd want more, that I could ask for more. That there was someone out there who might fit me. It honestly never occurred to me. Which is why I've been such a mess. Because we fit together, Oliver. You feel right. Like a pair of jeans that doesn't need to be stretched or shrunk. They just go on perfectly every time. It's weird that it happened so fast, but maybe that's what I needed. If it had happened slower, I might not have realized it was happening at all."

Oliver is quiet, his face neutral as I struggle to put into words all the feelings making my belly feel like I ate a beehive, but when I stop talking his forehead creases in confusion.

"You might not have realized what was happening?"

"That I was falling in love with you."

CHAPTER 34

OLIVER

I blink a few times. Kate holds herself still, palms spread on her thighs. She's so brave, and she's been through so much, and I can't imagine what she must have gone through to be able to stand in front of me and say that. So I respond the only way I possibly can.

"I love you, too."

Her face crumples, and I wonder if it's odd that I think she's just as lovely when she's crying as any other time. I get to her in one big step, wrapping her up in my arms, letting her soak my shoulder as I rain kisses down on her soft, loose hair.

"Is this okay?" I ask. "I just need—"

"I know," she says wetly. "It's okay."

We stand there, pressed together until I feel her taking deep, even breaths of air. She pulls slightly away.

"I swear I'm not usually this much of a crier. I blame the hormones."

"Sweetheart, you can cry on me anytime." Her face is close, and blotchy red, and my heart is full from loving her so much that I can't not kiss her.

She tastes salty and a little like the balsamic reduction on the caramelized Brussels sprouts. It's my favorite thing on the menu, so I lick into her mouth greedily. Underneath it all, she tastes better than the best meal, finer than the finest wine. I could live on her alone.

Kate meets me in intensity, her tongue curling and licking around mine and I can't believe she's giving me a chance, that this might be my life now. I groan when she sweeps her tongue across my bottom lip and suddenly everything in me is telling me to set her on top of the little metal desk and snake my hand up her silk-smooth leg, under her skirt and—

"Oliver!" Her tone is less lust-addled and more admonishing.

I yank my hand back guiltily. "What?"

"The restaurant. Your parents."

Her lips form a berry-red pout. I can't resist pressing another kiss to them.

"I forgot." I really had. Nothing is more important to me than the success of this restaurant—except for the woman I'm holding onto for dear life. I'd gladly grab her hand, escape out the back door, and drive to Vegas to get hitched tonight, the rest of the world be damned.

She must see something of my half-baked plan in my eyes because she shakes her head. "No."

"But—"

"You can't do that to Nat."

Fuck, she's right. Her being right is probably something I should get used to. It's not like I'm not already used to the women in my life knowing everything. "Okay, I'll talk to Nat and she'll understand that I need to take off early. We can go wherever you want."

"You know what?" Kate scoots off the desk. I see her visibly straighten her spine into that ready-to-take-on-the-world posture I've come to know and love. She's about to do something wonderfully brave. "Let's go tell your parents we're having a baby."

* * *

We tell my parents. They're suitably shocked for about twenty seconds and then by some unspoken communication they both melt into puddles of goo at the idea of another grandchild. When Kate tells them we're together without being detailed about it, they welcome her with almost embarrassing eagerness.

I'm certain they'd given up any expectation of me settling down. I think I'd done the same.

But settle down isn't even accurate. I'm not settling for anything when it comes to Kate, that's for sure. She steadies me, but I'm not settling. Not by a mile.

I can tell Maman wants to have a nice long get-to-know-you chat with Kate, but I tell her there's plenty of time for all of that, appeasing her with the promise of brunch tomorrow. Then Kate accompanies me as I make the rounds, making sure everyone is happy and things are running smoothly. I keep hold of her hand, but she doesn't seem to mind. She smiles and jokes, the consummate hostess. Even so, after a while I can tell she's wearing out, not to mention she never got to eat dinner. I put in a special order for her and return her to her friends.

Ricky gives her a querying glance. "Everything okay, Kate?"

"Everything is good," she says. It's a simple statement, but it seems to mean something to Ricky because he grins, then leans over to shake my hand.

"Welcome to the family, Oliver."

Ricky's acceptance is a balm. "Thank you."

"Oliver, the food is amazing, this place is amazing, you are amazing," Nicole says. "And you've got the most amazing woman in the world right here."

"I know." Their approval means a lot. My chest feels stretched with pride.

"We're going to take off soon. After Paris, I'm still not on California time. Kate, you need to crash at our place tonight?" The question is innocent but Nicole's tone is not.

Kate glances at me, her eyes twinkling in the light. She's showing none of the ambivalence I've seen from her in the past. I already knew how strong she is, but I'm starting to realize how powerful she can be when her strength is used in service of something she really wants instead of something she's trying to protect herself from. She licks her lips. I remember what they taste like and my blood heats like I've been set over a power burner on Mercy's stove.

"No, thanks," she says, holding my gaze, heat and love and promise emanating from those bewitching blue irises. "Oliver will take care of me."

Oh, yeah, I'll be taking care of her, in every way I can. And the fact that she's going to let me—that means everything.

Nicole giggles and Lani snorts. "I'll bet."

I'm saved by the arrival of Kate's food. It's kouraine, something Chef Jamila adapted from my mother's mother's own recipe. It's wholesome and nourishing and everything I want for Kate, for our baby, for our relationship. I want them to thrive.

Kate takes a bite, closes her eyes, and moans. Just like that, I'm back on the carrying her out of here train, but I bide my time. She needs to eat.

Her eyes finally open. "This is the best thing I've ever eaten in my life."

"Eat up, Kate. I'm going to make another round. See you in a bit."

Her hand finds my arm and squeezes. "Thank you."

I drop a kiss on the corner of her mouth, my heart too full for words.

* * *

The party goes on for too long after that, but eventually people start filing out. Nat looks dead on her feet. My parents kiss and hug me and Kate and confirm our brunch plans for tomorrow. Ricky and Nicole blow kisses and wave. I see Nicole whisper something to Kate and give her a tight hug before Kate collapses into a chair.

I visit the kitchen, where everything's winding down, and shake Jamila's hand reverently. "You are without equal. You did it."

"We did it," she counters. "And now we only have to do it every night for infinity."

"Isn't it great? I'll see you tomorrow." Tomorrow, when the doors open to the public for the first time, is probably more critical than tonight, but I have confidence in my staff, in the menu. There will be some kinks to work out, but we'll handle them. I can't be too worried when I have Kate waiting for me.

I've never had someone waiting for me to stop working before. It's going to be an adjustment to institute more regular working hours. There's so much to figure out. But I know we will. It's been an unconventional path, but I feel so lucky to have ended up here.

When the last of the revelers are gone and the servers have cleaned up and clocked out, and the kitchen staff has prepped and cleaned and signed off, Nat, Kate, and I are the only ones left.

Nat and Kate have been talking in hushed tones, each with her feet propped up on a chair. They look like they've come to some sort of understanding, heads bent toward each other as if they've known each other a lifetime instead of a few hours.

They look up at my approach, identical expressions of mischief in their eyes.

"Oh God," I groan. "Why do I feel like I'm in trouble?"

"Don't worry, boss, we're only plotting a little. It's for your own good." Nat swings her legs off the chair and stands up, cracking her back audibly.

Kate laughs, the throaty chuckle quickly becoming my favorite sound. "You make it sound so sinister. We're just same-paging about practical matters."

"Such as?" I hold out my hands for Kate to take and gently pull her to standing. Once she's upright, I don't let go.

"Dates and times and places and people," Nat says. "You know, all the stuff I deal with so you don't have to."

"And don't think I'm not grateful. Now, you go sleep. Tomorrow's another big day."

"That it is," Nat says. "Kate, I'm so happy this one found you. Really. I'd lost hope he'd ever form a functional adult relationship. You've restored my faith in humanity."

"Jesus, Nat, don't scare her off."

Kate just laughs. "Well, the functional part remains to be seen. But I'm glad he found me, too. And believe me, I'm glad he's got you." They trade hugs and kisses the way girls do even if they just met, as long as they've decided they're going to be fast friends. Together, we walk to the back door, locking up behind us.

"I'm off. Don't stay up too late." Nat throws us a leer, then drives off in the sporty two-seater she bought herself for her last birthday. I forced her to book a rental for the weekend, so I know she doesn't have a long drive; otherwise I'd be worried about her at this time of night.

I turn to Kate. "Where are you parked?"

"At my hotel. I got a cab here."

"Then allow me to drive you to your hotel. Which one?"

"The Biltmore," she says with an airy toss of her head.

I unlock the Mercedes, help Kate into the passenger seat. "That's convenient, since that's where I'm staying."

"I know. I was sort of hoping I could bunk with you. If you've got room."

"You're welcome to, but I have to warn you—there's only one bed."

"Sounds perfect."

CHAPTER 35

KATE

It's a repeat of the night of the wedding. We're both a little nervous, both exhausted after an epic day. Both not exactly sure what's going to happen next. But this time, I'm not beating myself up over wanting to find out.

We pull up to the hotel in Oliver's SUV and hand it over to the valet. I retrieve my bag from the bellhop and we find Oliver's room, the main feature of which is the king-sized bed. We take turns in the bathroom, showering and changing into our pajamas, then brush our teeth side by side, me poking only a tiny bit of fun at Oliver's charcoal toothpaste.

Oliver sets the alarm on his phone so we'll have plenty of time to get ready in the morning before we meet his parents for brunch.

"Your mom and dad seem really great," I say as we climb under the plush duvet, trading pillows until we're both satisfied with our level of cushioning.

"They love you already," he says. "It must run in the family. The Merciers fall in love with Kate Treanor at first sight."

"You didn't," I scoff, scooting back until my back is nestled against his front and one of his arms wraps securely around my middle.

"I did," he argues. "I saw you dancing and I knew you were going to change my life."

"I'll concede that I've definitely changed your life." Getting knocked up is pretty much the definition of a life-changing event.

"It's not just that." His hand splays across my abdomen, cradling the rapidly expanding swell of flesh there. He kisses my hair. "You would have changed it regardless. Did you know how happy I was when I saw you at the wedding? I couldn't wait to talk to you again, to get your number, to—"

"Get me back in bed?" I finish dryly.

"If possible," Oliver admits. "Did you know I haven't slept with anyone else since I slept with you?"

"Since the wedding?"

"Since the first time."

I had no idea. "Why not?" I whisper.

"I'm not exactly sure." He's always honest, which I love but sometimes hate. "I was preoccupied with the restaurant. But on some level I think I knew it would take me a long time to find anyone I wanted as much as you."

I turn around so I can see his face. "Really?" It could be flattery. Flirting is second nature to him, after all. But he's got me, in his life and in his bed. He doesn't need flattery. In fact, he sounds a little stunned at his own admission. His eyes are dark and focused on me, his eyelashes obscenely thick and long.

"Really." His voice is grave. "I'm not the smartest man in the world, but I have learned to listen to my instincts. From the moment I saw you—those instincts were activated, Kate. I didn't have a chance. And now I want to belong to you, and you to belong to me. In a totally progressive, non-creepily possessive way, of course."

"Of course." I can't help my half-smile. He's a bit of a caveman, but at least he's self-aware. Who knew I'd dig that particular combination?

"You've given me this incredible gift."

I wrinkle my brow, not sure to what he's referring.

"You've given me a chance to earn it. To deserve you. To make you happy."

"Oliver, listen to me." I want him to hear me, really hear me, so I stare at him hard. "You don't have to earn this. My love is not conditional. If I've learned anything over the past few years it's that love isn't finite. It goes on and on, even if you wish you could stop loving for just a few minutes because sometimes loving hurts so much."

A familiar pang zips through me as I recall Ben's face. I'll never stop loving him. I'll never stop hurting. But that's not going to stop me anymore.

"If I've learned anything over the past few months, it's that as strong as I thought I was, being with you has taught me that true strength isn't about being an untouchable skyscraper that stands on its own. It's better to bend sometimes, to lean on something or someone else. It feels better. It gets me further. It makes me happier. So you're already making me happy, Oliver. Just by letting me in, by being patient with me, by not giving up on me. By giving me someone to find pleasure in, and hope with, and plan for the future with. I never thought I'd have any of those things ever again."

He kisses me fast and fierce. "I love you, Kate."

It feels strange to hear that in the voice of someone else. But it feels good, too. The words warm me from the inside out.

I know I don't have to say it back, but I do anyway, and his tender smile in response is worth it. I kiss that smile, but halfway through it turns into a yawn.

"It's been quite a day," I whisper, snuggling deeper into the pillows facing Oliver. He strokes my hair lightly, his body a comfortable weight to relax into. I think we both wish we had enough energy to act on the sexual tension we've been stockpiling. But I'm wiped out.

"One of the best days of my life," he whispers back.

I don't know if I'll ever get used to his relentless romanticism and unabashed emotions. Maybe it's better if I don't. Then every day I have his love will seem like a small miracle. Or maybe not so small.

"Oliver?"

"Yes, Kate?"

"If you set your alarm for half an hour earlier, we could go to sleep right now and still have time for other activities in the morning."

"I already factored that in," he says, only a little smugly. "You're not the only one who can make a plan. Sleep now, Kate."

And I do.

* * *

Eight hours later, we're in our hotel bathroom's glassed-walled shower, wet and slippery with soap.

"Right there, oh, yeah, that's it. Don't stop." My moans echo off the tile and glass walls.

"There? Damn, Kate, you're so tight."

I shudder and lean into his touch. "Yeah. That feels so good."

"That's it, tomorrow I'm booking you a standing weekly appointment with my masseuse in Koreatown."

"I won't say no," I manage, as Oliver's clever fingers dig into the meat of the muscles in my lower back, then travel to my hips. He's been massaging me for about ten minutes, and I'd feel guilty about all the water we're wasting except it all feels too staggeringly good.

I brace my hands against the wall of the shower as Oliver stands behind me, working his magic fingers into the fleshy rise of my hips. The tip of his semi-hard cock brushes against my damp skin and I shiver despite the temperature of the water.

He's been a perfect gentleman since the alarm woke us, arms pressed against each other, feet tangled together. I appreciate being allowed to fully wake up before sex, but now I'm done being patient.

Quickly, I turn around. I wrap my hand around Oliver's length, press my breasts to his chest and attach my mouth to his. He feels so good against me, solid and safe. I've always felt a little unsteady having shower sex, like I'm one misplaced bar of soap away from a head injury, but with Oliver I feel completely secure. He's got me. And he's got me so turned on with his tongue working its way into my mouth and his hands coming up to cup my breasts, flicking at the sensitive tips. I want to spear myself on him, shove his cock between my legs and sink down, not caring if I'm wet enough.

I'm done denying myself.

In lieu of shoving him into me, I take the tip, slide back the foreskin and nestle it against my clit, rub it through my folds. He groans, and shifts so he's sliding through my slickness, the pressure on my clit in conjunction with the friction of his cock making me even wetter than I was before. Still, it's not enough.

"Oliver, I need more."

"Hang on, darling." He kisses me, then turns me around to face the shower wall, placing my hands against the tile in imitation of my earlier position. He crowds around me, his chest to my back, kissing my shoulder, one hand anchored on my waist. The other hand snakes around and rubs my clit with a practiced motion that makes those nerves light up like Fourth of July sparklers. "Okay?"

I nod, and force out a breathy, "Yes."

He makes a cross between a laugh and a moan at how desperate I sound.

His cock drags up the cleft of my ass as he lines up behind

me. My hair hangs wet and heavy around my face as I wait, trembling, for him to push inside. I know it's going to feel good, but I'm not prepared for how excruciatingly slowly he goes, breaching me one fucking inch at a time. I'm about to slam myself back and take everything I want, but his hand digs into my hip.

"Wait." He sounds as wrecked as I feel, so I obey, holding myself still as he continues his slow glide to my center. When he's finally there, he doesn't move. I'm overwhelmed with how full I feel in this position. My aching need hasn't abated, but his stillness allows me to concentrate on how amazing it feels to be joined together so deeply.

When he finally starts to move, long slides almost completely out and then firmly back in, I let him control the pace. I hinge forward, keeping myself planted as every muscle in my body responds to the firm thrusts and matching pressure against my clit.

I'm hypersensitive, aware of a million sensations all at once, of him filling me up, of the water raining down on us, of Oliver's tender words in my ear. I'm beyond forming words of my own, but I absorb his *sweetheart, love, beautiful, so good* until my orgasm sneaks up on me with the flick of his finger against my sensitive nerve cluster and I convulse around him. His answering groan tells me he's coming, too, and then he folds himself over my back, his mouth on my shoulder, breathing hard.

I'm twitchy and sated and still keyed up when he slips out of me and we shakily wash the evidence of our lovemaking away.

I turn off the tap. The silence at the cessation of water fills the room conspicuously.

Water drips from Oliver's beard onto his chest, rosy with exertion. His cock hangs full between his legs. He's beautiful and he's mine. He steps out of the stall first and wraps me carefully in a towel before he takes one for himself.

"Best shower ever."

"I'm trying not to think about all the water we wasted."

I twist my hair up in a second towel. I'll have to work extra hard to get it looking presentable before meeting up with his parents. I hadn't fully thought through having an ex-supermodel as a sort of mother-in-law. If Aziza, as she insisted I call her, hadn't been so gracious to me last night I'd be an even bigger ball of anxiety right now.

"Hey, it didn't go to waste," Oliver argues.

"I suppose not." I stick my head out of the bathroom to take a look at the time. "Oh shit, we've got to hurry."

"You know what, we've done enough rushing around. Let's take our time."

"But your parents—"

"They'll wait. We're giving them a grandchild, after all."

Still, I rub my hair vigorously, trying to get most of the water out before I start combing it.

"That particular get-out-of-jail-free card is only going to work for a little while, I hope you know."

"I know, but I'm going to milk it for as much as I can in the meantime."

I stop what I'm doing to stare as Oliver puts on deodorant. The simple yet intimate act strikes me hard. This is happening. I'm with a guy. I'm *with* Oliver. He's my...lover? Partner? Father of my child? All of the above. And more.

"You okay?" he asks, catching my gaze in the mirror.

"Yeah," I answer slowly. "I'm okay. I'm good. I'm great, actually."

He smiles at me, that wicked rogue's smile, complete with dimple, that snared me all those months ago. The smile of someone who knows what he's offering is worth the trouble to get it.

"You're right. Now that we're here, there's no rush."

We've got the rest of our lives, after all.

Kate Treanor and Oliver Mercier invite you to a family-style New Year's Eve Party

Mercy Restaurant
Eagle Rock, California
7PM
Festive dress

EPILOGUE
KATE

New Year's Eve

Despite feeling conspicuously front-heavy as I walk into Mercy, the surprisingly becoming silver maternity dress I splurged on proves worth it when Oliver leans close to me and whispers how beautiful I am.

We've invited our closest friends and family to a private dinner party at Oliver's flagship restaurant. They think they're here to help us ring in the new year, but that's not the only reason. Oliver's mother, father, brother, sister-in-law, and nephews flew in for the holidays from New York. My parents came, as did Kelly and Chris, and Riley, too.

Ricky and Nicole are here, and the Never a Brides, of course, Ophelia, Rosie, and Lani, complete with plus-ones.

Nat's here, with her new girlfriend, and Darsh, my assistant-turned-right-hand man who's helped me expand my podcast slate as well as plan for the day coming very soon when I'm going to be taking a maternity break.

The restaurant has been converted for the evening into a private dining room with two long tables. The wine is endless, and since I'm so close to my due date, I'm even allowed a glass. The food is unparalleled, as always.

When Oliver gets up and stands in front of the fireplace, no one pays him any attention until he whistles sharply and the crowd turns to him.

"Thank you all for coming tonight. It was important to Kate and me to have you all here, all in one place, before the baby arrives and we're too exhausted to have adult conversations. Thanks to my family for coming all the way from New York, and thanks to Kate's family for coming all the way from the Valley." The group laughs. "Kate, you want to join me up here?"

I nod and heave myself out of my chair, unable to keep the sappy smile off my face. I know what's coming and they don't.

"Kate once accused me of being in love with a fantasy. She was wrong—I was in love with her, and I knew she wasn't perfect. But she was right, in a way, because our life together has far exceeded my wildest fantasy."

"That's sweet, I think?" I say, laughing. My heart is light because I know just what he means. Neither of us is perfect, but what we have together is pretty darn close.

"You've all met my cousin, Michael. He's going to say a few words."

Michael, a minister at a progressive church in the Bronx, gets up, takes out his notes, and comes to stand between us in front of the fire. Oliver holds my hand in his, and there's a murmur as some people in the crowd recognize the age-old tableau we're making.

"Good evening," Michael says. "We're gathered together to witness the joining in matrimony of Oliver and Kate." Now the murmurs are louder, mixed with a few gasps and sniffles. I glance across the room as a mixture of shock and excitement ripples through the guests.

"Surprise!" I say, and everyone laughs. "We're getting married."

"Right now," Oliver clarifies.

Our parents knew, but we didn't tell anyone else, not even the Never a Brides. I've had enough wedding planning to last me for a lifetime, so Oliver arranged most of tonight. The ceremony will be short and sweet, but before Michael can get to the good part, there's a strange feeling at the base of my swollen abdomen. First a cramp, then a gush. I stare down at the puddle on the floor and my ruined shoes. "What the fuck is that?" I hear myself say.

Oliver's voice breaks through my almost willful obtuseness. "Your water broke, Kate."

"But I'm not due yet."

He stares at me, wonder, anticipation, and a hint of fear in his eyes. "I don't think the baby cares about that. He's coming."

I'm about to protest and say he can jolly well wait until after we finish the ceremony, but that's when my very first contraction smacks into me like a searing brand across my midsection. "Holy fuck, that hurts." This is happening. I grip Oliver's hand tightly. Rosie's in front of me in a flash, smiling and saying reassuring words. This might be my first rodeo, but it's not hers.

"Well, friends," Oliver says, "it seems we'll have to reschedule the ceremony. Our son apparently likes a surprise even more than we do."

* * *

Our baby arrives in the early hours of the brand new year, changing our lives yet again. Oliver swaddles him and lays him on my chest, wrinkled and pink and cranky. He's lovely.

"So, what do you think?" Oliver asks quietly. "Does he look like a Ben?"

I've been thinking about this for months, ever since Oliver first brought up naming him Ben. A part of me wants to honor my first love, the first man I thought I'd spend the rest of my life with. But as I gaze down at the tiny being I grew and birthed and now get to hold and feed and love, I know I don't need to. Ben wouldn't want me to. He'd want this baby to be his own person. He'd want him to forge his own path. I've made peace with the fact that I'm honoring Ben by continuing to live my life, and I've been blessed with so much richness.

"What about Maverick?"

"Maverick?" Oliver frowns. "It's not French."

I laugh. "No, it's not French. Or Irish. It's Californian."

"So it is." Oliver kisses the baby's nose, then mine, then grins. "Maverick it is."

"He's already got a mind of his own," I say a bit grumpily, "stealing our wedding thunder."

"Wonder where he gets that from?" Oliver teases.

"The three of us are going to keep each other on our toes."

"I hope so." Oliver sighs, sounding content with his lot in life.

Maverick buries his head against my chest. I'm swiftly learning that at mere hours old he can already communicate that he's hungry and Mama better deliver the goods. My nipples are sore, but I'm told they'll toughen up. I grimace as he latches on. Never thought I'd look forward to having tough nipples.

Sore nipples and wedding-crashing baby aside, I can't complain. I've stopped fighting against my feelings. It turns out life is so much better than I ever thought it could be.

* * *

* * *

Thank you so much for reading! If you want to go back in time to when Kate was still acting, scan the code to download the free prequel to my Sawyer's Cove: The Reboot series starring Kate herself!

xoxo,

Libby

ACKNOWLEDGMENTS

Author's Note: While this book takes place in the real city of Santa Barbara, California, and various parts of Los Angeles, the locations are fictionalized. Kate's podcasts are the product of my imagination, but those she references and shares with Oliver are real. Check them out for some great listens!

This book, like every other, was a team effort. Thanks to those who helped turn it from my scribblings into something beautiful and readable: Brian Calvert of Calvert Illustrations, Sue Khodarahmi, Sara Kettler, and Dylan Osborn. All mistakes are mine.

Thanks for the advice, expertise, and sanity preservation techniques of Pippa Baker-Rabe, Lena Eson Roe, Anne-Catherine Fallen, Monique St. Paul, and everyone at CTRWA. I'm constantly inspired by my amazing students at the Westport Writers' Workshop—you are all rock stars! Thanks for the head checks and encouragement of my plotting group, Isabel Morin, Annette Nauraine, and Kate Kettler.

Thanks to my two babies, who aren't babies anymore. Being a mom has taught me so much about myself and is the best/hardest job in the world. I drew on my own experiences to write Kate's pregnancy, and am grateful for the chance to revisit that period in my life through this story.

And thanks to my mom, who taught me everything I know about being a great one.

ABOUT THE AUTHOR

Libby Waterford is the author of the Sawyer's Cove: The Reboot and the Never a Bride series. She's obsessed with her pollinator garden, DIY fermentation, and writing swoony first kisses and hopeful happily ever afters. Her steamy contemporary romances mix witty banter and all the feels with a solid dollop of good old-fashioned sexual tension. Libby wrangles her two ever-growing sons and a husband in Fairfield County, Connecticut.

Get a free story at libbywaterford.com and email her at libby@libbywaterford.com.

- facebook.com/LibbyWaterford
- instagram.com/libbywritesromance
- bookbub.com/authors/libby-waterford
- goodreads.com/libbywaterford
- amazon.com/author/libbywaterford
- tiktok.com/@libbywaterfordauthor